# STOPPERS

*Aliens in Hallywalooly*

## Richard M. Davidson

**RADMAR Publishing Group**

ISBN-13: 9780997638172
ISBN-10: 0997638176

Cover design by: Yash Raut on Unsplash and Richard M. Davidson

Printed in the United States of America

*This novel is dedicated to my grandchildren as they choose their careers, in the hope that their achievements will contribute to a healthier Planet Earth and increased knowledge of our Universe.*

# CHAPTER 1 – FIRST SOLO

Malcolm (Mac) Blackwell viewed the patchwork Florida landscape and the distant horizon from the open door of the skydiving plane. He had seen this vista from 10,000 feet before, seven times, the first two as he prepared for tandem jumps harnessed to an instructor, and the last five preceding jumps when he and an instructor descended as a pair of individuals. This was the big one, number eight, his first solo jump. Mac would be the last jumper to leave the aircraft. He was as ready as he could be; an analog altimeter on his wrist and a backup audible altimeter, a Dytter, tucked into his helmet. He had originally set the Dytter to emit beeps at his intended chute-opening altitude of 3,000 feet, but at the last minute he had reset it to 3,500 feet for more time in case the beautiful view caused him to lose focus and ignore his wrist device.

From a point behind his right shoulder, Mac heard his instructor, Roy Ryan yell, "Time!"

Mac grasped both edges of the open doorway and launched himself forward, thinking, but not shouting the traditional *Geronimo* exclamation. As he parted from the aircraft he thought he heard Ryan yell, "Watch your body position!"

The freefall was exhilarating. Mac spread his arms and legs to add extra area to his body for flight control and scanned the ground beneath him while he tried to tune out the wind noise. It was a beautiful afternoon, but he knew his jump would be the last today for this skydiving company, because a front was due to pass through the area soon.

*What was that noise? OhmyGod! It's Dytter time already, 3500 feet from the ground.* His wrist altimeter arrow was entering the yellow section, 3,000 feet. He pulled the chute release.

The colorful rectangular canopy billowed above Mac, but he instantly realized all was not well. *Ryan said I needed to watch my body position, and I ignored that. My head was too low, and my shoulders weren't level. I wasn't symmetrical, and now the chute lines are twisted.*

Mac tried to check his wrist altimeter, but the twisted lines had him spinning in circles beneath the canopy. He could see he was in the red danger zone, but he couldn't read numbers. He didn't think he had time to cut the main chute free and open his reserve chute, so he tried something he had read in a skydiving magazine. Mac brought the risers together, squeezed them, and rotated them in the direction opposite to his spin rotation. His spin slowed and gradually stopped. Success. Then he felt a jerk, and looked up at his canopy. More problems.

At lower altitude, Mac had dropped into turbulent air from the oncoming front. The canopy partially collapsed, and he drifted off-course toward some woods and wetlands. He pulled on every line he thought might help, but he had only minor influence on his drift direction.

Mac's thinking raced, and everything seemed to slow down. As a kid, he repeatedly experienced bad dreams in which he died in a car driven over a cliff. This was pretty much the same thing. He wondered what his family would think. They had warned him his skydiving could end up with him dying in a horrible accident. Now they'd be able to say, "I told you so" even though he wouldn't be around to hear it. He might as well go out with as much style and as little damage as possible.

He pulled a riser to aim as best he could for a swamp. The shallow water would cushion his impact a little bit. The canopy was spilling more air, and it was starting to rain. His descent accelerated. His feet hit the water and pushed into the thick vegetation at the bottom of the swamp.

Then, amazingly, the vegetation pushed aside, and Mac continued to fall into an open space beneath the swamp. He hit something soft when he landed, and he had clean air to breathe.

As he came to rest, Mac yelled, "I'm alive! Hallelujah!"

A voice nearby answered, "Not Hallelujah. You are in Hallywalooly."

# CHAPTER 2 – HALLYWALOOLY

The mysterious voice called to others somewhere in the darkness, "Pull in that parachute, reposition that vegetation mat, and replace the lost swamp water. Lights will remain off until that entrance is hidden again."

Mac heard sounds of activity all around him, followed by several sequential shouts of "Secured." Lights went on, and he realized he was in a huge cavern. Mac examined the soft surface beneath him, and discovered it was similar to the inflated cushions used by stunt people in movie-making.

The person who apparently owned that first disembodied voice approached Mac. He had red hair and was wearing a light brown version of bib overalls as were others in the background.

"Welcome, Topper; I will take you to our medical unit to be sure you were not hurt by the impact."

"My name's Mac Blackwell, not Topper, and I think I'm in good shape. What is this place?"

"I already told you. You are in Hallywalooly, and I called you Topper because you came from the top world. Everyone here is either a Topper, a Dropper, or a Stopper. You will learn about Droppers and Stoppers later. As to your condition, we have a formal requirement that every new person receives a medical examination."

"I'm pleased that your hidden entrance to this place saved my life, but I'm certainly not going to stay here. Don't call me a new person like a recruit. Why do I need an examination?"

"To put it into terms that a Topper will understand, we want to avoid any legal problems if you are damaged in any way."

"I guess that's reasonable. Do you have a name?"

"You can call me Red. I have a more complex designation, but Red will do for now."

"Good enough, Red; where do I go for this required examination?"

"I will take you there. Climb onto this utilizer and hold onto the railing."

The utilizer resembled a green baggage cart with handrails in the front and middle, providing stable grips for the driver and up to two standing passengers. Red toggled switches on the front handrail to activate it. He said, "Forward." The vehicle moved swiftly and silently toward the far end of the cavern until Red said, "Turn left." At that point the utilizer entered a smaller side tunnel. Three minutes later, it came to a halt in a second, smaller cavern chamber. By the time they stopped, Mac had discovered that the utilizer vehicle followed a pattern of wires embedded in the stone floor. When Mac mentioned his observation, Red said, "We can use voice commands to direct a utilizer in tunnels where we have wires in the floor, but we use search mode or manual controls in rougher areas where there are no wires."

Red led Mac into a brightly lit room cut into the cavern sidewall where a person wearing a red lab coat and a disheveled-looking older man awaited them.

# CHAPTER 3 – EXAMINATION

The woman in the lab coat gestured for him to sit down and spoke briefly with Red, who left the room and drove away on the utilizer vehicle. She turned back toward her seated patient.

"I understand that your name is Mac Blackwell and that you entered Hallywalooly on a rapidly descending parachute."

Mac didn't want to be impolite, but he felt it necessary to assert himself. "That's correct. I'll be forever grateful that your entrance under the swamp saved my life, but I intend to leave as soon as your examination is finished."

She nodded. "It is a bit early to discuss the schedule for your leaving. First, relax and let me check your condition."

"Are you a doctor?"

"I am a healer."

She touched Mac's shoulders and neck, and he felt a soothing feeling of warmth spread through his body. His muscles relaxed, and he visualized himself floating on an inner tube in a lake he had visited as a child. He couldn't remember when he had last experienced such peace and relaxation. He moaned favorably and said,

"You are indeed a healer. I haven't felt this well in years. I'll have to come back to Hallywalooly periodically for additional treatments."

She moved her caressing hands to Mac's head. "You do not still want to leave us, do you?"

He hesitated while her suggestion saturated his thoughts. "Not really, but I don't know anything about this place and you people. Do you live here, or is this your workplace?"

The healer smiled, rested her hands on Mac's cheeks, and then swiveled his chair so that he faced the older individual who had remained silent up to this point.

He said, "Welcome to Hallywalooly, Mac Blackwell. My name is Jablesh, and I will answer all your questions."

# CHAPTER 4 – JABLESH

Mac's eyes scanned Jablesh, trying to extract a first impression. The older man with his wrinkled brown robe, sandals, and shaggy beard fit Mac's expectation for a biblical prophet who had overslept, or a homeless person. He remembered his mother's admonition not to judge a book by its cover. Mac, still feeling great warmth from the healer's work, sat back in his chair and waited for his orientation session. *Why had he never felt so calm before? This must be what it meant to be at peace with oneself.*

Jablesh's voice was surprisingly strong for his apparent age. "You have had a climactic introduction to Hallywalooly. We do not get many Toppers from the above-ground world, but most of them have similar sudden entries through sinkholes, underwater vents, or mining shaft collapses. We are an underground society located mainly in Florida, but we also have small outposts in many other regions of Earth. We live in places where subsurface water carves out caverns. We have been here longer than most of the people who live on the surface – for thousands of years,"

"How could that be? How did you get here? Your ancestors had to come from somewhere else."

"The Ancient Ones did. They came from a distant planet where they lived underground because of their planet's poisonous atmosphere. An asteroid impact fractured one of their planet's moons, sending chunks of that moon into the planet, collapsing the surface and sending poisonous atmosphere into the underground dwelling levels. Most of the population died, but the remainder abandoned the planet on twelve spacecraft. One of those spaceships reached Earth. Once the Ancient Ones settled here, they interbred with early natives to increase their numbers and continued to practice underground living. Florida was perfect for them. The whole peninsula lies atop limestone that dissolves over time due to subsurface water, forming caverns that can be more than a hundred feet across and high, and miles long. That limestone is also suitable for tunneling to interconnect the natural statewide caverns and for smoothing of the stone floors and walls."

"If it's not too personal, Jablesh, how old are you?"

"We do not count years of age like the surface people, because we do not wear out and die."

"That sounds impossible. All of Earth's creatures have an expected lifespan."

"Logical, but even though we are interbred, our heritage from the Ancient Ones is dominant, so, like them, we do not die of natural causes. We are not among Earth's creatures in the sense you used. We can, of course, be killed in accidents."

"Why don't you make yourselves known to people on the surface?"

"They are too aggressive and warlike for us to be comfortable with them. We do make contact with them when necessary, but we keep them from realizing our presence. You will learn more about our goals and missions in later discussions."

"But you said today that while surface scientists have spent centuries looking for life on other planets, beings from another planet have been living beneath their ground for a long time."

"That is true."

"Why don't you look different from surface people?"

"I told you, we interbred with indigenous Earth people. Their appearance was dominant over ours, while our longevity was dominant over theirs."

"Wow! That's the best of both worlds."

# CHAPTER 5 – AGRICULTURE AND LAYOUT

Mac had turned to skydiving because he had neither a romantic connection nor a job. His picture frame company, started after he returned, wounded, from an Army tour of duty in Afghanistan, went bankrupt at the hands of many overseas competitors, and his girlfriend, Maxine, traded him in for a bank vice president. It had been fun going to parties as the Mac and Maxine duo, but he knew now that a long-term romance requires more than novelty. Anyway, given these two strikes against his opportunities in the surface world and his wonderful feelings after the healer's work, it hadn't taken much for Jablesh to convince Mac to stay in the underground world, at least for a while.

Mac's next orientation step was a tour and quarters assignment conducted by his first friend, Red. He and his utilizer vehicle were waiting for Mac when the meeting with Jablesh ended.

"Hello, Red, I see you're expecting me. You didn't think I'd be leaving right away."

"Jablesh is quite persuasive. I cannot remember the

last time a newcomer turned him down."

"Where do we go next?"

"First, I will show you one of our agriculture areas, and then I will take you to your assigned sleeping quarters."

"That sounds good to me. Food and sleep are two of my favorite things."

"Thanks to the healer's work, you will not have the frequent food cravings that you did on the surface, but you will have a schedule for eating and sleeping."

They emerged from the small connecting tunnel into the largest cavern Mac had yet seen. On one side, water ran down its walls into large ponds from which sprays of water arced over a wide area of assorted green vegetable plants and fruit trees. Dazzling overhead lights filled the chamber with the brilliance of sunshine.

Mac smiled his approval. "This is all very impressive, Red."

"The topsiders have only recently discovered aquaponic agriculture, but we have been using the same techniques for a very long time. It has been a natural development here because our main resource is water. The ponds contain fish which we eat for protein and which add waste to the water. The fish waste in the water becomes fertilizer when it is sprayed over the plants. The bright lights take the place of sunshine, the one resource we don't have underground."

Mac tried to determine the type of lighting unit being used, but he couldn't because of the distance. "You said you've used this approach for a long time. Can you estimate how many years?"

"That is an interesting question, but I understand

it. We also use our various types of lighting to alternate day and night, so we have the same understanding of a day and a year as topsiders. I would say we have been doing this for at least two hundred years, probably longer. Before that, we raised our plants on the surface and brought them down here at harvest time. As the surface population increased, we decided we had to grow everything in the caverns so our society would not be discovered."

"Where did you get your lighting and mechanism technology? The surface world couldn't have done this so long ago."

Red laughed. "I am sure Jablesh told you that our ancient ancestors came here long ago from a distant planet. Even in those ancient days, they had technology. Otherwise, they never would have arrived here. Different sections of the universe have widely varying stages of development."

"Then, you think there are other beings in the universe beside your Ancient Ones and our Earth people?"

"I know there are. The Ancients recorded their encounters with other beings before they arrived here."

"Wow! I feel as though the whole nature of the universe just changed for me."

"Be logical, Mac. You grew up on the surface, where you saw stars in the sky at night. You looked at those stars as though they were sending you light while you watched them. The truth is that you were seeing light emitted millions and billions of years earlier because of the stellar distances and the time it takes light to travel that far. Does it not make sense that the planets around those ancient stars developed life forms that, because they were so much older, would be more advanced than those on Earth?"

"When you look at the possibilities that way, it does feel reasonable. Thanks for changing my point of view, Red."

"It is time to take you to your sleeping quarters. You have had a long and eventful day."

Red directed the utilizer down a different small tunnel and then branched off to enter a tunnel with many small chambers along its length. "Traveling is quite easy now, but it took many years for us to smooth the floors of all the tunnels and to widen narrow passageways."

Mac said, "You know all the twists and turns around here. Will I get a map so that I'll understand the complete layout of these caverns?"

"There will be a computer screen on the wall of your sleeping chamber. Just ask it for the map layout, and it will be displayed. Anyway, we have arrived. Your temporary quarters are in the chamber marked with three red dots above four yellow dots. Depending on your future assignment, you may move later."

"There's no door for privacy."

"We do not use doors. No one will enter without authorization. There is a turn in the hallway to block out unwanted light. Get some rest, and I will come for you in the morning."

# CHAPTER 6 – SLEEPING QUARTERS

Mac entered the chamber and was surprised to discover it had familiar furnishings including a rather large bed, two comfortable-looking chairs, and a chest to hold all the personal possessions he didn't have. When you arrive by parachute, you travel lightly.

A female voice said, "When we receive a new Topper, we give him or her a chamber with furniture that will feel familiar and comfortable. You will change to one with Hallywalooly styles later."

Mac turned to see a dark-haired woman who had entered from the next room. "Thank you. Are you the maid?"

"Similar sounding word, but not quite; I have been assigned to be your mate. I am Merrilong."

Mac tried to be cool and hide his shock. "Merrilong is a lovely name, and you are quite attractive, but I'm not looking for sexual favors. I'm not even sure how long I will want to stay here. For now, I just want to get some sleep and then learn more about Hallywalooly."

"Mac Blackwell, for as long as you are in Hallywalooly, you need to have a mate, and not only for sex or procreation, although those activities may come later." She lifted her upper garment to reveal a port mounted in her side. "I will install a port like this in your body so that we will be able to share our bloodstreams as we sleep. The tubing device connecting the ports will deliver blood with our characteristic of eternal life to you, while blood from your body will give me new stamina and strength that I need because of our many generations of inbreeding. I will be a good mate for you, and we will share our life stories."

"Then, this sharing of bloodstreams bonds me into your society?"

"It does that, and it bonds me to you and you to me for life."

"You don't have marriage or divorce here?"

"Those are strange words to me, Mac Blackwell. What do they mean?"

"Let's leave them for a future discussion, Merrilong, but please call me Mac. If we are to be mates, even for a short time, we can't be formal with each other."

"We are now mates, Mac. Remove the top of your jumpsuit and shirt. Then sit on the chair while I install your port."

# CHAPTER 7 – DROPPERS AND STOPPERS

The next morning, Red arrived to drive Mac to a meeting chamber where he would have additional discussions with Jablesh. Merrilong said she would obtain clothing in the Hallywalooly style and other supplies for Mac while he was gone.

The overnight two-way transfusions between Mac and Merrilong must have had their predicted effects, because the two now looked upon each other as though they had been mates for a very long time.

Jablesh greeted Red and Mac upon their arrival at the meeting chamber. Red then turned to leave, but Jablesh said, "Do not go. You will be a contributor to today's discussions, along with a few others I have invited."

As they sat waiting for the others to arrive, Mac asked Red, "Is Jablesh the overall leader of Hallywalooly, or does he report to someone else?"

"We do not have a rigid structure or organization chart, but Jablesh is given great honor because he was asked to guide us by the last direct descendants of the

Ancient Ones before they departed to continue their search for additional life forms and habitable planets."

"He must be very old."

"We do not keep records of age, but Jablesh looked the same when I was a child, and my father told me the same thing. When you do not have to worry about a limited lifetime, age has little meaning."

"Are your parents still alive?"

"No, unfortunately they died when a new sinkhole opened up, sending many tons of surface rubble into the caverns below it. That is our most common cause of death here."

Jablesh led three other individuals into the meeting chamber, and they all joined Red and Mac at the large round table.

Jablesh nodded his greeting to all of them and opened the discussion. "Thank you for coming. It is time to give Mac Blackwell, a Topper who is our most recent addition, a better understanding of Hallywalooly social structure. He has committed to us by beginning the bonding procedure with his mate, Merrilong. Red has told him that our society is composed of Toppers, Droppers, and Stoppers. While that is not strictly true because of cross-breeding among those groups, it will do for an introduction to our people. Mac, do you have any opening questions?"

"As you said, I'm a Topper, which is clearly someone who came here from the surface world. Will I be surprised to learn what Droppers and Stoppers are?"

Jablesh glanced at the others. "I suspect you will. Right now you are in the presence of members of both of those groups. I will start with Stoppers, a group which includes Red and me. Stoppers are descended from the Ancient Ones who stopped here in their search for planets where their life forms could settle and dwell. They had offspring with indigenous humans, so actually Stoppers have some Topper ancestry. I am a fourth generation Stopper, while Red is a twenty-third generation Stopper. I am much older than most people here, but my functional abilities have not diminished with age. Red's formal designation is Guardian S2357. He is the fifty-seventh member of the twenty-third generation Stopper group. Obviously, it is easier to call such a person by a unique characteristic – in this case, his red hair. Red, do you wish to comment on your name or ancestry?"

"I will add that all those in my generation group do not have similar genetics. Some have more ancestral breedings with Toppers than others, who may have bred more frequently with other Stoppers along the generation sequence. Jablesh is the closest I know to being a pure Stopper."

Jablesh laughed. "Pure in heart and goals, but not perfect in any way."

Mac said, "So far, I've seen that Toppers contribute to their own group and also to the Stopper lineage. Are Toppers involved with Droppers too?"

Jablesh said, "Absolutely. These two men and this woman seated across from you are significant Droppers. Allow me to introduce Benjamin Franklin, Orville Wright, and Eleanor Roosevelt."

"But they're all dead and from greatly different time periods."

"They were dead, but the Ancient Ones gave us the genetic key to unlimited lifetimes. Droppers are selected individuals whom we drop out of the bottoms of their coffins and revive by transfusing them with our blood of unlimited life. We can go after candidates by tunneling under gravesites anywhere on Earth. After revival, they help us with our missions, and we refill their coffins with the bodies of others who die here from accidents."

"I find that hard to believe. Mr. Franklin, are you able to work on new inventions, or are you limited to advising modern people?"

"You are right that I don't have my old drive in proposing new inventions, but I can work through problems, after I absorb the applicable changes in technology since my time."

Eleanor Roosevelt said, "Oh, Ben, you always were the expert in taking a common sense approach to problems. You won't have any difficulties with applying new knowledge."

Orville Wright joined in. "I'll help this old-timer catch up, and I thank you, Eleanor, for sharing your knowledge of jet aircraft and rockets. I could have done wonders with such power sources."

Mac waved across the table at the three famous people. "I concede my skepticism. You three are definitely ready to continue making contributions. Are all the Droppers famous people?"

Jablesh shook his head. "No, they are not all famous, but they all have useful talents."

"Can Droppers breed with others?"

"No. Droppers are revived after death, but they are not fully alive. They can be with us for many years, but they cannot procreate offspring. They can live with Stopper companions, but they are not able to become mates. Do you think you understand our society now,

Mac?"

"I do, but I wonder why you are spending so much time educating me, and I would like to learn more about those goals and missions you mentioned today and earlier."

Jablesh reached over and touched the back of Mac's hand. "Your interest is appreciated. We will discuss those topics at a future private meeting."

# CHAPTER 8 – MERRILONG

Mac drove the utilizer back to his lodgings with Red as the passenger. He was pleased that he remembered the route without requiring Red's coaching. After arrival, Red took the controls and left for his normal duty station.

Upon entering his quarters, Mac found Merrilong arranging his new clothing and supplies in the storage chest. "Hi, Merrilong. I see you picked up some goodies for me. Thanks for handling that chore."

Merrilong put her hand on his cheek. "In addition to clothing that is more in keeping with our styles, I brought back shaving supplies. I assume you will want to remain clean shaven, rather than grow a beard."

"I never was good at beards. My blond hair doesn't grow fast enough."

"It will grow even more slowly now. As our overnight transfusions start to extend your life expectancy, your body functions, like hair growth, will slow down. You are not going to age much at all."

"Does that mean that you're actually much older than my thirty-seven years? You're very attractive, regardless of your age, but I am curious."

"As you have already learned, we do not worry

23

much about age here, but I do have a considerably longer history than you. I hope that will not bother our relationship."

"I see you as a woman in her early thirties, and that's how I will always think of you. We've already slept together as mates with the mutual transfusion connection, but now, it's time to learn about our sexual compatibility. I'll want to change into one of the new garments you brought home for me anyway. They're not too different from the jumpsuit I wore over my jeans for skydiving." Mac removed his shirt and started to help her remove her tunic, caressing her breasts during the process.

Merrilong followed her tunic removal by assisting him with removal of his jeans and stroking his crotch. After some additional mutual visual appreciation and caressing, they headed for the bed, without the inconvenience of their overnight transfusion connection. After prolonged initial foreplay, Mac found that Merrilong anticipated his every desire and led him to multiple climaxes with minimal rest intervals. Completely aroused, he spent every bit of energy he had in his efforts to please her. Their sexploits seemed to go on forever. He had never had a partner so in tune with his needs and wishes. Mac thought he had satisfied her, but when they left the bed and dressed, he felt the need to ask.

"Merrilong, am I a good mate for you when it comes to sex? You've had more history and experience. I want you to be as satisfied as I was."

"Mac, everything was perfect. You are mine, and I am yours forever." She accentuated her statement by giving him a passionate kiss.

He responded with more caressing beneath her tunic.

"Mac, do you want to go back to the bed?"

"No, we've proved we're much more than compatible. We should do something related to teaching me about Hallywalooly."

"Where would you like to go? What would you like to see?

"First, I'd like to learn about the children of Toppers, Droppers, and Stoppers, and then I'd like to visit a school and see a group of children with different types of ancestry."

"Are you hinting that you would like us to have a child soon?"

"Not at all. Let nature take its course. I'm just wondering about the results of genetic mixing among the people with greatly different ancestries."

"I appreciate your curiosity, Mac. Sit down, and I will give you my understanding of such things."

"Aha! Merrilong is both my mate and my teacher. I'm ready to learn."

"I will start with the simple part. Droppers cannot have children because they were dead and have been revived to let us make use of their talents. They are not fully alive."

"They are alert; not like zombies. I've met some Droppers."

"They are not the living dead. They are revived formerly dead people. As such they interact with us on an equal basis, but they cannot reproduce, either with each other or with members of the other groups."

"Good. I understand and now only have to learn what happens when Toppers and Stoppers try to have children together."

"Mate of mine, that combination is just as easy to understand. The Ancient Ones from elsewhere in the universe mated with indigenous Toppers to produce the first Stoppers. Therefore, Stoppers may mate with Toppers because Stoppers have Topper genetics themselves. No matter how many interbreeding generations pass, Stoppers will always be able to mate with Toppers."

"Do the children always look the same?"

"Of course not. There are the same variations that there are in children born on the surface. A child's appearance depends on the genetic makeup of his or her parents, grandparents, and relatives in earlier generations. Appearance-wise, we are all like Toppers, but we have some characteristics, such as eternal life, from the Ancient Ones."

"What other characteristics did you inherit from the Ancient Ones, and will our children have them?"

"Good news! Now I know that you want to have children with me. I would like that too. Of course, our children will have all the characteristics I have inherited from the Ancient Ones plus your family's genetic traits too. You know about eternal life on my side. You will have to learn about other Stopper traits from Jablesh. I am not permitted to tell you."

"Even though you're my mate?"

"Especially because I am your mate."

# CHAPTER 9 – JABLESH

Mac felt surprised and honored when Red delivered Jablesh to his quarters the next morning. After their initial exchange of greetings, Jablesh instructed Merrilong to accompany Red on an errand so that he and Mac would have privacy.

After they left, Jablesh said, "Mac, today we will answer questions you have already raised, along with some that are just beginning to form in your mind."

"I believe you've already answered one. Stoppers and Toppers with Stopper blood transfusions are telepathic. You read my thoughts."

"I am from an early generation of Stoppers. Because I am genetically closer to the Ancient Ones, I have the ability to read thoughts at any time and at some distance. Others, like Merrilong, can only share nearby thoughts during a time of crisis. You will develop that capability as you continue to exchange transfusion blood with Merrilong."

*I don't know about that 'time of crisis' qualifier, but that explains how Merrilong anticipates my every desire during sex.*

Mac clamped down on his wandering thoughts to avoid them being detected. "My next question is one that is impolite, and I apologize for it in advance. I believe that you lied to me when you said that people with the eternal life characteristic die only in accidents. You should have many more people here if that were true. How else do they die in addition to accidents?"

"Thank you, Mac, for demonstrating that you are an astute thinker. I suspected and hoped that was the case. I will answer your question, but you must not share my answer with anyone else. I do not want my people to worry about unlikely problems. Do you agree?"

"I do, although you told me that in time of crisis, others may be able to read my thoughts."

"I will take that chance. We have reduced population, in large part, because when we use the transfusion process to revive a Dropper, the donors lose their immortalities and die within a few years. The revived Droppers also have a limited period of return from the grave. We also have many more tunnel and cavern collapses than we admit. Earlier, when we first arrived on Earth and mated with indigenous people, many of our number chose to live on the surface. There, they were subject to animal attacks and conflicts that decreased their numbers. However, there are still many Stoppers and their descendants secretly living among the Toppers."

"Jablesh, you said that you had missions to be undertaken for Hallywalooly. I suspect that people die while carrying out these missions."

"Our goal is to make the population of Earth peaceful, or at least less aggressive. The Ancient Ones could not foresee all of Earth's wars, but they set up our society in the hope that we could guide the people who live on the surface toward peace. We have been much less than successful so far."

"Have you had any accomplishments?"

"A few. Our people helped the writers of the Bible, both Hebrew and Christian sections. Some of them were early Hindus, Buddhists, Muslims, and disciples in other religions as well. We have found religion to be the greatest system for influencing the behavior of the surface people. During various wars, Hallywalooly agents influenced the intelligence services on both sides in ways that would lead to an earlier end of the conflict. More recently, they instigated the tearing down of the Berlin Wall and helped focus attention on Earth's accelerating climate change."

"Those are significant accomplishments that I would not have suspected."

"That is one of our goals, to guide the Toppers without their realizing they have been influenced. Regarding the parachute jump that brought you to us, we generated the turbulent air that redirected your landing spot. The partial collapse of your parachute was not caused by an approaching weather front as you assumed."

"That suggests that you wanted me, specifically, to land on your swamp entrance. Why me?"

"Your friend Maxine is actually one of our Topper agents. Her assignment was to identify a Topper who would fit in with our future plans. At this point, I will say that she did well in selecting you."

"Why didn't you send me an invitation instead of risking my life by making my parachute collapse?"

"Would you have believed Hallywalooly and space aliens existed underground if we had simply invited you?"

"Probably not, but wait a minute, Jablesh; Maxine

and I had sex many times, and I didn't see a transfusion port on her."

"That is because Maxine was not selected for coupling with a Stopper mate. We give only a few special Toppers the gift of unlimited life."

"Does she know about the transfusion mating process with a Stopper?"

"No, and if you should ever encounter her again, on the surface or in Hallywalooly, do not mention it. We do not want her and others like her to feel inferior."

"I understand. You're telling me that there are different classes of Toppers. Are there different classes of Droppers and Stoppers as well?"

"As I have already indicated, some Droppers are historical celebrities, while others are unknowns selected for their usefulness. Some Stoppers, like Red, are classed as Guardians. They are the closest thing we have to military people. Merrilong is a Stopper from a group whose primary assignment is to keep our society functioning smoothly, without being affected by external interactions."

"Does that mean that if you ask me to do something connected with the surface people, I won't be allowed to share that information with Merrilong?"

"No, she is your mate in every sense of the word. Share and learn from each other at all times. You will find her a reliable resource."

"I'm glad that was your answer. Now for the most important question, what do you expect of me?"

"I'll speak to that subject later. For now, charge your cell phone from the computer screen in your quarters, and Red will set up a temporary local relay tower so that you can use it to call surface numbers. I want you to explain your disappearance so people up there will stop looking for you. After that, come see me, for your first assignment."

# CHAPTER 10
# – SKYDIVING
# SCHOOL

Roy Ryan wondered whether he was about to be fired. Not only had he lost a student jumping solo for the first time, but because of a sudden burst of rain, Roy hadn't spotted where Mac landed after his chute problems. Everyone at the skydiving school assumed that Mac Blackwell had died, but none of the ground search teams had been able to locate the body. This was a major catastrophe and the first presumed death in the school's history. For now, Roy was restricted to minding the office while his associates instructed new students, some of whom were overly nervous because they had heard about Mac's tragic jump and disappearance. Roy's jittery chewing of his right thumbnail was interrupted by the loud telephone ring. *I know they have to keep that thing loud so we can hear it when no one's in the office, but the shock of it going off almost made me swallow a piece of thumbnail.*

"Skydiving Central, Ryan speaking."

"Hello, Roy, Mac Blackwell checking in."

"What! You just scared the shit out of me. You're

supposed to be dead. Where are you, and how did you survive?"

"I blew off course into some trees, and my chute caught on a branch, so I never hit the ground. I unstrapped myself to get down the last couple of feet. Then I was able to pull the chute down and pack it away. By the time I finished that, the rain was coming down hard, so I caught a bus on the road nearby and went home. I know I should have called in earlier, but I was busy."

"You were busy? Do you realize that we had emergency vehicles and ground search teams looking for your body for two days? You S.O.B., thanks to your presumed accidental death, we had a bunch of students drop out, and the word is already spreading on social media that we don't take safety seriously. You're going to cost us a bundle."

"Sorry, Roy, I was just happy to be alive. I won't be coming back for more jumps, but I'll arrange for you to get my parachute back. It may take a few days before you receive it."

"Keep the damn thing. It's unlucky. No one will want to jump with that chute again. Anyway, Mac, I'm sorry I got so angry. It's great news that you're alive. Any broken bones or serious injuries?"

"Nope, the tree scratched me a bit, but I'm already healing. I'm just not going to tempt fate by jumping again. Say hello to the others for me."

"Will do. By the way, you probably saved my job by surviving. Thanks for that. If I ever run into you again, I'll buy you a beer. Goodbye for now, you lucky bastard."

# CHAPTER 11 – TRAINING

Mac grinned as he tucked his phone back into his pocket. "That does it, Red. You can dismantle that temporary relay tower. No one on the surface will be looking for my mangled body anymore."

"That was a smart move. It is always good to avoid having dangling unanswered questions like what happened to you."

"Do you have a spare utilizer cart? I'm supposed to meet Jablesh in the healer's room."

"Take the yellow one. I will be using the green one to check out some overhead cracks in a side tunnel. If they foreshadow the development of a sinkhole, we will have to close that tunnel and drill an alternate one bypassing that area."

"Thanks, Red, I don't know how long I'll need this, but I'll bring it back as soon as I can."

"Do not worry about that, Mac. I will sign it out as yours for an extended period. I have the feeling that Jablesh is going to keep you on the move for quite a while."

Mac easily found his way to the studio where the healer had examined him earlier. He expected to find Jablesh there, but the healer told Mac that Jablesh had been delayed.

Upon sensing Mac's disappointment, she added, "His absence will not delay your training. He wants me to teach you a bit of the art of healing. He thinks you will need it."

Mac relaxed and sat down. "Before you start any instruction, please tell me your name. We were never introduced, and I'd feel awkward working with someone I couldn't address by name."

As she handed Mac a short sleeve red lab coat similar to hers, she said, "My name is Summerly. Extend your hands toward me, palms up."

Mac did as instructed and was surprised that she blew on his palms but did not touch them.

"They are good hands; a bit muscular, but still suitable for gentle touches. My breath has opened the skin pores on your hands. Now, I will increase their sensitivity with this special spray." She held an atomizer bottle above his palms and squeezed the rubber bulb to release an extremely fine mist with a satisfying but unidentifiable aroma.

"What is that aroma? I've never smelled anything like it."

"The spray is a formula handed down from the Ancient Ones, and the aroma comes from their home planet. You will use this spray, but you will not be qualified to apply it to others or formulate it."

"Will I have to return for a new application of spray every time I use these healing skills?"

"No, I expect one application to last for many months. The spray is only effective if it follows the application of a certified healer's breath. You are not going to be trained all the way to certified healer level. You will become a healer's assistant, a level which will still allow you to accomplish many things. Now, I will show you a demonstration and test."

Without warning, Summerly picked up a small knife and cut Mac's left forearm. Blood spurted from the wound.

"What did you do that for? I need a tourniquet and some bandages."

"Press your right palm gently onto the wound for several seconds. Then lift your hand away from the wound."

Mac followed her instructions, not knowing what to expect. When he lifted his right hand off the wound, there was no sign that the incision had ever happened. The wound was completely healed, leaving no scar behind.

"That's amazing, but what happens if I'm wounded in a spot I can't reach with either hand, like my back?

"Then you should place one palm on top of your head. You will have the same healing result."

"Will this procedure work if I apply my hands to someone else's wound?"

"Certainly. You are becoming a healer's assistant, extending my skills to your remote location. Treating someone else with one hand on top of the head will allow you to treat two people at once."

"Does the healing come from your skills or that spray from the Ancient Ones?"

"Both. The spray will not work unless its application follows my blowing on your palms. The healing skills must be passed from one healer to another. Someday, you may become fully qualified as a healer, but I think you will be too busy doing other things."

"What other things?"

"Here comes Jablesh to answer your questions. I will leave you now."

Jablesh entered wearing the same brown wrinkled robe as before. Mac wondered whether the old man had any other clothing.

Jablesh laughed. "Believe it or not, I have many robes, but they all look the same."

"You read my mind again."

"I did indeed, and I also saw that you are quite concerned about assignments that I might give you. I will try to clarify things for you. When I passed Summerly on the way in, she conveyed enthusiasm for your first efforts as a healer's assistant."

"She did that without speaking to you, of course."

"That is correct."

"It will take me a while to get comfortable with mindreading."

"Someday, it may save your life."

"Are you about to give me my first mission?"

"Not quite. It is time to explain why we wanted you to join us."

"Please do."

"We needed to add a Topper to lead others from Hallywalooly on missions to the surface. Those missions will be aimed at guiding the surface people toward important preferred long-term goals rather than fighting over day-to-day matters."

"I still have to ask, why me? I'm not wise to the ways of being a leader in physical or philosophical conflict."

"But you have shown bravery by jumping out of an airplane and staying calm under adverse conditions."

"I'll try to help on small specific missions. Don't expect me to change society."

"That is all I will ask of you."

"What's my first assignment?"

"We are going to try an approach to reducing violence in surface cities, and I want you to lead the first test effort. If it works, we will duplicate the attempt in other cities with different leaders."

"If it doesn't work, I'll probably be killed. The authorities in cities have tried just about every possible approach to reducing street violence. What makes you think a new try will work?"

"No one else can do what we are planning."

"I hope you're not going to send me into a dangerous neighborhood without backup."

"You will have as much backup as you wish, but I expect it will take only eight or ten of our people. Here is the plan ..."

# CHAPTER 12 – JACKSONVILLE

Mac sat in the box truck's passenger seat as they drove into one of Jacksonville's off-limits neighborhoods shortly after ten o'clock in the evening. He wore black jeans and a black hoodie sweatshirt so that his white skin would not be obvious in this black section of town. The driver, Preacher Clark, and the other nine Droppers in the back of the truck were all black. Continuous chatter filled the cargo compartment until Preacher pounded on the separating wall and yelled, "On the turf now." Then everyone became silent.

Without warning, a black trade van pulled out of an alley and blocked the street in front of them. Two tough-looking teenagers with handguns stepped out and shouted, "That's as far as you go. Kill the engine and get out."

Preacher turned off the engine. Then he and Mac slowly opened their doors and climbed down, leaving their doors wide open. The other nine Droppers quietly scurried out of the rear loading door and split into two columns, one on each side of the truck, masked by the open side doors. Mac retreated to the back of the line of men on his side.

One of the gang soldiers shouted, "Who are you

fuckers? This is our turf, and no one enters, without our say-so."

Preacher closed the truck door on his side and stepped forward. A huge Dropper called Crunch did the same on the other side of the truck. Preacher said, "This was our turf before it was yours. You were still being wet-nursed in those days. You ever hear of Preacher and Crunch?"

"Sure. They started our gang, but they died in a shoot-out with the cops. Must have been twelve years ago."

"I'm Preacher, and he's Crunch, and we're back to slam you. You kill anything that moves and some that don't. That's chicken shit. We were better than that."

"Don't know who you fuckers are, but they're dead, and you're gonna join 'em."

The teen fired four shots and hit Preacher and Crunch twice each. As they went down to the ground, two other Droppers moved in front of each of them to confront the younger men. Mac filtered past the others to rest his hands on Preacher's head to heal him and disintegrate the bullets. Then he went to the other side of the truck to do the same for Crunch. Having done his job, he dropped back to wait.

Preacher stood up, grinned and moved in front of the two Droppers masking him. Crunch did the same on the other side of the truck. Preacher laughed. "You can't kill us. We're dead already. But we'll come back to kill you and tear your insides out if you don't stop shooting civilians."

Two other toughs appeared from behind the van. They shot Preacher and Crunch again plus two other Droppers. Once again, other Droppers moved up alongside the truck to stand in front of their bullet-ridden buddies. Mac moved up on the driver's side of the vehicle and rested his healing hands on Preacher and the other man. Then he moved to the other side of the truck and rested his hands on Crunch and the other Dropper.

The four *corpses* rose up and faced the gang members. Preacher said, "We can play this game all night, but you ain't gonna do us no permanent damage."

The four teenagers stared at Preacher, Crunch, and the other two Droppers. Then, they stared at each other. The leader said, "What are you – zombies?"

"We're the living dead. We can come back any time we want to kill you, but you can't kill us. There are lots of us. We're unstoppable. Now get that van out of our way, and remember our message. Stop shootin' kids and family folks."

All ten of the Droppers stepped in front of the truck and glared at the teens.

The younger men got the message. They jumped into the van and drove off.

The Droppers laughed and climbed back into the truck. As they drove away, Mac said, "I'll round up some Dropper old-timers from their rival gang, and have the *zombies* confront them tomorrow night."

Preacher nodded. "Glad you learned your healer lessons well. I didn't enjoy dying from gunshots so much that I wanted to do it again and again. The young punks in these gangs will see zombies behind every wall and in every alley from now on."

# CHAPTER 13 – EVALUATION

Jablesh was seated at the meeting room table when Mac walked into the room. "How did your first mission go, Mac?"

Mac laughed. "I know you can read my thoughts, so that question is a mere formality. Everything went better than I expected, except for the fact that the gang bangers shot Preacher and Crunch twice instead of just once. They must have thought it could be a fluke to have them return from the dead once, but it was more serious if they did it a second time."

"Those young gang bangers are unpredictable. Preacher and Crunch were that way once, but our revival process for Droppers includes discipline and socialization training."

"I felt comfortable working with them, Jablesh. It almost slipped my mind that each of them was a brutal killer in his former life. The mission went well, thanks to fears of zombies incited by movies and video games, but I have a question regarding our objectives."

"Ask it."

"Preacher threatened the gang bangers with death if they didn't stop killing civilians, but why wasn't there pressure to stop killing members of rival gangs? That's not making the street thugs more peaceful."

"You are correct Mac. We made some progress, but we did not get to a final objective. We will repeat this approach, in other cities with gang problems, and hopefully reduce street killings substantially, but we have not succeeded in changing the leopard's spots, so to speak. Hopefully, the authorities in the surface cities will gain inspiration and confidence to take new steps to reform these young urban killers. Our program is only a first step to reduce their danger to society as a whole. We did succeed in another way."

"How?"

"We demonstrated that we can make an impact on surface society without anyone realizing that we were involved. If the gang members tell anyone what happened, they will be ranting about zombies, and no one will believe them."

"What about our Dropper gang crew? Did you revive them just for this confrontation mission? What happens to them now?"

"They are no longer the sinister street thugs they were when alive. When we revived them, we changed their outlooks and feelings of responsibility. They will continue to make valuable contributions to Hallywalooly in ways that have nothing to do with violence and gangs. They may work with you again and even become your friends."

"They already are."

"Strange; I could not read your thoughts on that one. As you continue to have blood interchange transfusions with Merrilong, you are becoming more complex."

# CHAPTER 14
# – MOVING

When Mac returned to his quarters, he found Merrilong gathering his possessions and hers into large containers. "What's happening? Are you cleaning everything?"

"We will make sure everything ends up clean, but our project for today is moving. These quarters are temporary ones, used for newly arrived Toppers. The rooms and furnishings are designed to remind newcomers of their homes in the surface world. You have become a reliable agent for Jablesh and have earned a more typical Hallywalooly home. Congratulations on the success of your first mission."

"You know the details of what occurred with those street gangsters? I've only now returned from sharing the results with Jablesh. I was looking forward to telling you all about our standoff."

"Do not worry about sharing the details with me, Mac. I learned from your thoughts that you were successful, but I do not know exactly what happened during your encounter on the surface."

"Jablesh told me that Stoppers can only read the thoughts of others during a crisis."

Merrilong's eyes sparkled. "Jablesh thinks he knows

more than he really does. What he told you may apply to some Stoppers, but not to members of my family. You are my kin now, so as we grow closer and continue to share our bloodstreams overnight, it will not apply to you either. I suggest that you do not reveal this information to Jablesh. Our secret may serve you well someday."

"I'm learning that there are many secrets in Hallywalooly and that only a few of them will be revealed to me. Now, tell me about our move."

"We will be going to a much larger home, which will be ours for as long as we want it. We will be in a side cavern all our own, and we will have our own aquaponic-style vegetable garden, polished granite floors, and plenty of room for your meetings and future children. Does that sound good to you?"

"It sounds very good, but do you expect me to be having many meetings there?"

"I do, but we will discuss them later, after we are settled. For now, I want to hear the details of your surface adventure."

# CHAPTER 15 – RED

After Red helped Mac unload the last of Merrilong's containers into the front room of the new cavern dwelling, they sat on a step for a rest and chat session.

Mac patted his friend's shoulder. "Thanks for all of your help. This rest break gives us a chance to talk a bit more. You're usually running back and forth between assignments and activities."

Red nodded. "They do keep me moving. That is part of the routine for a Guardian like me."

"Why do you have the title of Guardian? Are you guarding Hallywalooly against possible invaders?"

"We guard against danger of any type. We were posted to welcome you when you arrived by parachute, but we also continuously inspect tunnels and caverns for flaws that may lead to development of sinkholes, rockslides, or collapses. We also modify or open up additional caverns as they are needed by Hallywalooly. Unmodified caverns need smoothing of floors and walls plus elimination of stalactites and stalagmites. Living underground protects us from weather, except for some flooding, but we have to care for our structures just as you need to maintain buildings and roads on the surface. We study surface life in our schools, so your old ways are familiar to us."

"Speaking of my old ways, I would always appreciate drinking a beer after a tough job like moving. Does Hallywalooly have beer?"

"Hold that thought. I will return in five minutes."

When Red's utilizer vehicle returned, it carried ten glass containers filled with a dark liquid. Red handed one to Mac. "Try this."

Mac was surprised by the familiar, yet different, taste of the drink. "It tastes like root beer, but a bit stronger."

"Root beer was originally made from the root bark of the sassafras tree. That is no longer the case because your people learned sassafras is poisonous. We have access to all kinds of roots, and we are immune to poisons. You are too, now that you are mated to Merrilong. What you are drinking is fermented root beer made from sassafras root bark."

"I like its sharpness. It's like drinking spicy beer. Getting back to you, does your Guardian position give you a particular rank or prestige?"

"No, but I enjoy responsibility. We do not worry much about ranks here, but we appreciate learning how to do things and applying our knowledge for the common good. That gives our lives purpose, especially since we live much longer than the Toppers from the surface."

"Apparently, I'll be in that longer life situation now that I have nightly transfusions with Merrilong, but we don't think much about lifespan on the surface. Most of us simply take life one day at a time. Do you have a mate or family, Red?"

"To some extent, all Stoppers are family due to cross-breeding over the centuries, but I have a mate, Flowerling. We have decided not to have children but to enjoy each other in harmony. We have a joint hobby.

I bring home interesting rock samples from Guardian excavation assignments, and she studies them and records information about them. Most people think of a cavern as having uniform rock walls and formations, but she has developed classifications for many different types of rock found here."

"All the females here have beautiful names that evoke peaceful thoughts: Merrilong, Summerly, Flowerling."

Red agreed. "They are all very special, and they make us males feel special too. How do you feel about Merrilong, Mac?"

"No other woman has ever made me feel so unique or has been focused more on my well-being."

"Mac, you are now one of us and part of that harmony I mentioned. We are all family."

# CHAPTER 16 – NOAH'S ARK

The first meeting at Mac and Merrilong's new home came two weeks after they completed their move. Red stopped by to help with preparations and arrangements.

"Jablesh asked me to help you with any advance needs for a meeting here tomorrow. There will be nine people attending, including the three of us. I suspect that a new major project is involved."

Merrilong looked amused. "It must be something new. Jablesh is infamous for omitting females from his conferences. I think he is afraid of us for some reason. Apparently, this project is important enough to include those who have been avoided."

Mac said, "The fact that he's holding the meeting here suggests that this project is going to be my next assignment. I hope it's something manageable and not too grandiose. Red, do you know who else will be coming?"

"In addition to the three of us, there will be Jablesh, my boss who is the Guardian in charge of construction, Preacher, Crunch, and two other persons. Jablesh did not identify them. He has been known to invite extra people at the last moment."

Mac smiled. "I asked Jablesh whether he would have

other assignments for Preacher and Crunch beyond dealing with surface street gangs. This must be what he had in mind when he said I might be seeing them again. What will we need for the meeting, Merrilong?"

"We should have food ready in case people get hungry or there is a break in the meeting. We should have drinks too."

Mac turned to Red. "Be sure the drinks include that fermented root beer you gave me earlier."

"I will. Would you like coffee too?"

"You have coffee in Hallywalooly?"

"We raise coffee plants aquaponically. They are short plants rather than bushes. I do not drink coffee myself, but I know most Toppers and Droppers like it."

"You talked about harmony in this society. True harmony requires coffee. Please be sure we have it for the meeting and that this house has the root beer and coffee at all times."

Red and Merrilong exchanged glances. Then, Merrilong said, "Mac Blackwell is truly at home now. He makes demands rather than accepting all things as they come. It is fortunate for him that I learned how to roast and grind beans to brew coffee when I was younger."

Mac smiled and realized he would enjoy the big meeting, whatever its subject matter would be.

The next morning, Mac and Merrilong stood at the entrance to their home to welcome the meeting guests. The green utilizer arrived first, bearing Red, Preacher, and Crunch. Mac was surprised when Crunch spoke as they entered, "Nice place you have here. With the right shoes, I could slide across that polished granite floor doin' fancy dance steps."

Mac laughed. "Good to hear from you, Crunch. You usually let Preacher do the talking for both of you."

"He talks in public – leader stuff. I do relaxed chatter."

Preacher said, "Crunch talking is a sign that we're all friends now. No need to put on the tough faces no more."

Red started to respond, but he was interrupted by the arrival of his boss, Guardian S2141, otherwise known as Shorty for obvious reasons. Shorty drove a more rugged version of a utilizer that had larger solid ribbed rubber wheels for traction in construction areas.

Shorty gestured over his shoulder. "The others were right behind me. They were not moving as fast as I was. Hi, Red. Introduce me to your friends."

Red performed the requested introductions, completing them as a purple utilizer arrived, bearing Jablesh, Ben Franklin, and Eleanor Roosevelt.

After exchanges of greetings, Merrilong and Mac, as hosts, invited everyone into the meeting room. The table was triangular, with seating arranged to have Jablesh, Shorty, and Mac at the three table points. Mac took a container of hot coffee before he sat. Several others also took drinks, including Preacher and Crunch who signaled approval after trying the fermented root beer.

Jablesh opened the meeting after everyone sat. "Good morning and welcome to all. This meeting is larger than most because I have a new project to suggest, which is also quite large. Most of you have had at least some exposure to the Bible, used by several religious faiths on the surface. In the early Hebrew section, sometimes called the Old Testament, there is the story of

Noah who built a ship called an ark and used it to rescue pairs of all the existing animals in order to save them from a huge flood. He was rescuing them so that they wouldn't go extinct. I want to do the same thing without the ark. Earth is going through a climate change ordeal that is endangering many species and driving some to extinction. We have underground colonies in many places on Earth. I want to use them to round up small groups of endangered species and take them to safe caverns. Our underground caverns are essentially immune to climate change and have a moderate temperature of between fifty-four degrees and seventy-two degrees Fahrenheit all year round, depending on their location. Except for rare cases, that should suit most species. What are your reactions to this proposal?"

Shorty gestured for attention. "This would be our most ambitious project yet. I assume you asked me to attend because you expect us to construct special holding caverns under many regions of Earth."

Eleanor Roosevelt said, "The caverns would be the easy part of this project. I've always been a champion for the environment and its impact on people. I've said that conservation of land and conservation of people go hand in hand. This project of yours would require a very large number of people to feed and care for the creatures we rescue, not to mention those who would have to raise or otherwise procure food for them all. We might have to set up a committee to study these issues before we start this program."

Ben Franklin laughed. "Eleanor, you speak like the diplomat you were when you lived topside. Poor Richard in his Almanac would say, 'Nothing ventured, nothing gained.' Too many people discuss things to death before they try to do them. I suggest a pilot program with the rescue caverns being constructed within Hallywalooly."

Mac agreed. "It amazes me to have the privilege of sharing thoughts with Eleanor Roosevelt and Ben Franklin. I'll have to side with Ben for a pilot program. However, Eleanor is absolutely correct that a worldwide program is extremely ambitious. Perhaps, we could turn this into a network of local efforts, loosely coordinated, in order to keep it practical."

Merrilong, seated next to Mac, patted him on his shoulder. "I agree with Mac to develop plans on a local basis, but I suggest that the first step should be to identify the species that would be involved. Are we talking about one hundred, one thousand, or ten thousand? Would most of them be the size of elephants or insects? Research is required."

Preacher contributed, "Wonder if old man Noah did research? Pictures I've seen only show big animals on the ark."

Jablesh said, "I hear enthusiasm or at least openness to studying this program. We have some time, but not a lot of it, before the likelihood of extinctions becomes critical. Many species have already disappeared from the surface world. I agree that the required effort will be huge, probably too much for one individual to handle. Therefore, I recommend that Ben Franklin and Eleanor Roosevelt coordinate the program. You both tackled immense problems when you lived on the surface."

Ben and Eleanor exchanged whispers. Then Ben said, "We'll do it, but we'd like Orville Wright to be our first assistant. He wouldn't want to be left out of things. I see him as returning to the surface and flying to the various local underground colonies to coordinate everything."

Eleanor added, "I'd like to see his expression when he first flies on a jet. He'll be thrilled."

Jablesh pushed his seat away from the table. "This has been a good first meeting. Shorty, you will assist Ben and Eleanor because you know about all the operations here in Hallywalooly and in the other Earth colonies. Red, you will take over some of Shorty's normal responsibilities here. Preacher and Crunch will care for the animals and other creatures for our pilot program here. Mac and Merrilong, thank you for the use of your meeting room. We'll soon have other projects for you."

Mac felt relieved that he wouldn't have a leadership role in such a large program. Merrilong liked the implication that she would soon be working with Mac on a different project.

# CHAPTER 17 –
# HOME SWEET
# HOME

"Well, Merrilong, our new home is a big success."

"How is that, Mac Blackwell?"

"Our meeting room worked well for a large and important gathering, and Crunch enjoyed our polished granite floors for dancing. By the way, now that we're mates, do you take on Blackwell as your last name? That's the way they generally work it on the surface?"

"We do not use last names in Hallywalooly."

"What if you had two other Merrilongs as friends? Wouldn't it get confusing when you were all together?"

"No. We would simply call each other Merri1, Merri2, and Merri3."

"Why wouldn't you call each other Merrilong plus the number?"

"Mac, have you not noticed that our tradition is for females to always have three syllable names? You know Merrilong, Summerly, and Flowerling; those names all fit the pattern. With three Merrilongs, we would shorten the name and add a number to keep the sound pattern. We live with water all around us in these caverns, so we suggest a rippling stream with our female names."

"When you put it that way, it's quite logical and beautiful too. I still have a lot to learn about Hally-walooly and its traditions."

"I thought our triangular table worked out well for the meeting. I arranged it to have the three most likely major speakers at the corners with their close associates next to them. Of course, I made sure I was next to you."

"That was a good touch, and you made a thoughtful suggestion about needing some research first. How do you like the kitchen in our new home?"

"It is much better than the one in our temporary quarters. There we had only one food spot, and we could only warm fresh food. Here we have three food spots. We can warm food or cool it to two different temperatures for different food items."

"What are food spots? Do you mean appliances, like an oven, a refrigerator, and a freezer?"

"I read about those. They are what people on the surface use, but they take up too much space. In our kitchens we simply have one or more ceramic slabs set into a counter. We secure our food to it and make it the temperature we want. We do not need to store large quantities of food because we have an automatic food delivery every day plus a garden for fresh vegetables. Each morning, I simply tell my computer screen what I want for the day, and it arrives within an hour."

"I think I understand, Merrilong, but how do you heat and cool the food if it's not in an enclosure like an oven or a refrigerator?"

"The food spot slab can invert. When we want to heat solid food, we rotate the slab so that the food is facing downward. A microwave beam below the counter strikes the food on the bottom of the ceramic food spot. When cooking is complete, the slab inverts, so that we have access to it. For liquid food, we leave the food on the top surface and heat it through the ceramic slab. We cool food facing upward on the food spot by varying the velocity of air blowing on it after expansion through a nozzle. Air blown through a nozzle and allowed to expand becomes cold, and the cold air cools the food quite quickly. It also removes any surface bacteria. Our old quarters did not have the cooling air device, so we could only heat food. Here we have three fully equipped food spot slabs, so we can cook or chill up to three things at the same time."

"I like the fact that the food spots take up so little space. I also feel that our bed here is more comfortable."

"Mac, you get better beds with special quarters. I have never had such a fine home in all my time here. It is because Jablesh thinks you are special, and so do I."

"After that remark, it's time for us to enjoy that comfortable bed." Mac led Merrilong out of the kitchen.

# CHAPTER 18 – OBSERVATIONS

The following morning, Merrilong noticed that Mac had risen early without waking her. She didn't see him in the kitchen, so she assumed he had gone out, perhaps to meet with Red. As she was preparing her breakfast in the kitchen, she heard sounds coming from the meeting room. She looked into that room and saw Mac walking from his assigned seat to that which Jablesh had occupied yesterday.

A bit puzzled, she asked, "What are you doing, Mac?"

"I didn't say anything, but during the meeting, I sensed several different streams of thought in Jablesh's mind. I couldn't decipher them, so I pretended I only heard what he said. Today, I'm trying to remember what I sensed. We Toppers have an old expression, 'Don't judge a man until you have walked a mile in his shoes.' I'm trying to focus my memories by sitting first in my seat and then in his. It probably won't make things clearer for me, but it's worth a try."

"I also sensed that he was thinking about several different things beyond focusing on the meeting. Jablesh's mind is very powerful, so I did not think it unusual."

"I think the reason I couldn't latch onto his thoughts is that for some of them, he was thinking in a strange language."

Merrilong looked concerned. "I did not pay enough attention to sense that, but if you are correct, there may be a problem. When Jablesh wants to hide his thoughts from others who are capable of reading them, he thinks in the language of the Ancient Ones. He is the only person left who understands that language and who can speak and think in it. He does not use it unless he feels something is very important and that it must be hidden from everyone."

"I'm certain it had nothing to do with his Noah's Ark program. Another interesting point is that he could have gone into much more detailed discussions of the new program, but he was content to cut the meeting short at the earliest convenient time. Something is definitely bothering Jablesh."

"The next time I am near him, I will try to read his thoughts. I am more sensitive to them than you. He may get careless and think in English or one of the other languages I know."

"Merrilong, you continually surprise me. I didn't know you were multilingual. How many languages do you understand?"

She was happy that she had impressed Mac. "I am only good at seven or eight languages. Some of my friends know many more. Summerly, the healer knows almost all the Earth languages. She absorbs the language of each person she heals."

"That is impressive. As a healer's assistant, I wonder if I will absorb other tongues when I treat people who speak languages other than English."

"You may, but I'm not sure. I've never discussed healing principles with Summerly. She likes to be mysterious and not discuss her work unless she is pressed to do so by Jablesh."

"Has Summerly ever healed Jablesh?"

"I see what you are thinking, Mac. I do not know the answer to your question, but it is possible that Summerly healed Jablesh at some time and absorbed his knowledge of the language of the Ancient Ones."

# CHAPTER 19 – PILOT PROJECT

Mac left home still wondering about Jablesh's hidden thoughts, but he switched his thinking to current matters when he saw Red driving a heavy-duty utilizer similar to Shorty's vehicle.

"Hi, Red; I see you have a new steed to drive. Is it Shorty's or is this a second one of the same type?"

"This is the backup unit to Shorty's construction utilizer. It normally sits unused unless there is a breakdown of the other one. The meeting at your place gave me a promotion to Shorty's normal job while he works on the new program. It is supposed to be a temporary assignment, but I think that conservation assignment for Shorty will last a very long time."

"Well then, congratulations on your new position. Do you get paid more?"

"You still have a few things to learn about Hallywalooly, Mac. We do not need money here because we can simply requisition anything we require for our responsibility or our personal desires. Merrilong has been taking care of requisitioning for your requirements. We only get money when we have an assignment requiring interactions with the surface people."

"Have you had such assignments?"

"We sometimes have small groups of Guardians go topside to help with relief efforts after natural disasters like floods and hurricanes. No one notices us among the large number of volunteers who help out at those times. If someone starts asking about us, we simply disappear and come back here."

"Have you heard anything from Shorty? Has he started on the new program?"

"He has been tunneling into a previously unused cavern about five miles from here. That one will be used for larger land animals. After he completes that job, he will create large depressions in the floor of an adjacent cavern for fish and aquatic animals. He will need two of those, one to be filled with fresh water and the second to receive salt water. The salt water pond will require piping to connect to the ocean underwater plus a safety valve system to keep the ocean from flooding our caverns. Shorty has many large efforts on his schedule."

"When I talk with you, Red, I learn more about Hallywalooly and I get news about current events too. Do you know about any other new projects involving Jablesh?"

"Even our pilot conservation project requires huge efforts. I hope Jablesh is not going to require us to work on other large efforts before this one has been completed."

"Agreed. I don't know about other projects, but I thought you might."

"No, I have been too busy covering Shorty's normal responsibilities to look for extra work."

Mac took the hint about how busy Red was. "Thanks for the chat session. I have to do some errands for Merrilong now."

Mac drove his utilizer to Summerly's healing studio. Unlike Red, she appeared to be relaxed and open to receiving a visitor. Mac entered and spoke to attract her attention. "Summerly, I had spare time, so I thought I'd check something with you. As a healer's assistant, am I supposed to stop in for further training?"

"No, Mac, if you get an assignment that requires additional procedures, I will train you for them as you prepare to leave. You do not need a new application of the special spray yet. Your healing capability should be good for another month or two."

"I have a question. Merrilong says that when you heal someone who speaks a different language, you absorb the ability to speak that language. Will I absorb a different language in the same way?"

"You will, Mac. Proper use of healing skills requires the ability to understand your patient and for the patient to understand you. You are not likely to encounter the different language situation in Hallywalooly because all Stoppers know English, and we teach it to Toppers and Droppers who don't already know it. I could enlist you to be one of the teachers of English, but Jablesh has other plans that will keep you busy."

"Do you know what his plans for my next assignment are?"

"I do, but Jablesh will have to be the one who informs you."

# CHAPTER 20 – ASSIGNMENT

When Mac returned home, he approached Merrilong to ask her where Jablesh lived. Before he could ask the question she said, "I do not know, Mac. I assume he has a private cavern of his own, but he keeps it secret. He would be bothered by many petitioners wanting favors if they knew where he lived. He initiates contacts with us, and we respond to him."

"Merrilong, I will never get used to your answering questions before I ask them. You can read my thoughts, but I am only beginning to be able to read yours."

"I apologize if I threaten your Topper tradition, but it saves time to simply answer your thoughts. You will soon become proficient at it as we continue to share our bloodstreams while sleeping."

"We have a saying on the surface that no man can understand a woman's thinking."

Merrilong smiled. "I said that you will become better at reading my thoughts, but I did not say that you would understand why I think the way I do. Getting back to your earlier thought question, why do you want to know where Jablesh lives?"

"Summerly told me that he has a new assignment for me, but she wouldn't tell me what it is."

"You will have to wait for Jablesh to tell you. He cannot be rushed."

"Merrilong, you are a very patient person."

"Patient, loyal, loving, and dedicated to you. Do not try to rush what happens in Hallywalooly. We have been here a very long time, and our life rhythms are those of Earth itself. This is a lesson that you will soon learn as one of us."

"I'll try, but that may be my most difficult lesson."

Merrilong cocked her head at an unusual angle. "It is hard for me to believe, but your inquiry to Summerly may have made developments move more rapidly. Jablesh is at our entrance, waiting for permission to enter. I sensed his thoughts. Now let us be polite and greet him."

Following the ritual greetings, Jablesh said, "I do not want you to be bored by inactivity, Mac. I have a new assignment for you. Join me in your meeting room to discuss it. Merrilong, please come with us. You will be included in this project."

Merrilong was surprised and delighted by the thought of going on an assignment with Mac. She knew they would work well together.

Being a group of three individuals, they sat at the three points of the triangular meeting table, Jablesh choosing a different point from their last meeting, presumably to indicate that one point was not superior to the others.

He first addressed Merrilong. "This will be a surface world project. I believe it will be your first visit there. Do you have any qualms about going?"

"Certainly not. I will be with Mac, and he will guide me at all times."

Jablesh turned to Mac. "How do you feel about taking Merrilong on a surface adventure where she may feel out-of-place?"

"I doubt that we'll have problems. We're a couple, and we work well together."

"Good. Your assignment will be to visit NASA at Cape Canaveral, take the facilities tour, and learn as much as possible about their plans for future missions to Saturn's moon Titan."

Mac frowned. "This sounds like a great first adventure for the two of us working together, but couldn't we get that information by using a computer to search the internet?"

"That would get us publicly released information. We need to learn whether competition of different missions for budget will make exploration of Titan a definite program or simply a wish list item."

"And why is Titan important to Hallywalooly?"

"Mac, you and Merrilong will have to promise not to share my answer with anyone before I give you that information."

They both agreed and swore themselves to secrecy.

"We need that information because when the Ancient Ones left Earth to find additional suitable dwelling places, one of their spacecraft found Titan to be promising. The passengers on that ship established a colony on Titan similar to Hallywalooly. If NASA explores Titan thoroughly, that colony will be discovered. We will want to convince NASA that their exploration of Saturn's moon is not important. If they do send an unmanned vehicle there, we will have to give the colony advance warning, so that they may prepare to sabotage the mission."

Mac said, "The colony on Titan can't be that similar to Hallywalooly. We have Toppers, Droppers, and Stoppers. Since there was no humanoid preexisting life on Titan, they can have only Stoppers. Their Stoppers wouldn't be able to intermarry with indigenous people because there weren't any. Therefore, the Stoppers on Titan are purebred Ancient Ones."

"Excellent analysis, Mac. I'm impressed. It is important to preserve that colony because their population is our only link to the original Ancient Ones."

Merrilong's face bore an unusual expression as she asked Jablesh, "When will you want us to go?"

Jablesh rose as he answered, "Whenever you feel ready within the next two weeks. I do not want to rush you, but it is important that we initiate this project in a timely fashion." Upon completing this statement, Jablesh bowed to Mac and Merrilong, and left their home.

Mac turned to Merrilong. "I saw your expression when you asked that last question. You have a problem with something Jablesh said, and I now know that you have the ability to hide your thoughts when it is important."

She smiled. "You are learning that I have a few talents I have not revealed to anyone. My problem with Jablesh's presentation is that he obviously has been in communication with this other colony. How else could he know they exist? They settled on Titan shortly after the Ancient Ones left Earth, many centuries ago. That means that Jablesh has been communicating with the Ancient Ones and their descendants for all that time. No one in Hallywalooly has known he could do that."

# CHAPTER 21 – DEPARTURE

As they prepared to leave for Cape Canaveral, Merrilong examined the clothes Mac had requisitioned for her. "Are you sure these outfits are what female tourists wear? They are unusually colorful and they don't cover as much of my body as I consider normal?"

"Actually, they cover more of your body than is typical for a tourist woman, because I needed to hide your transfusion port. That would attract unwanted attention."

"This will be fun, going somewhere else with you."

"Keep that in mind, Merrilong. You will be accepted as a tourist if you appear to be having fun and are optimistic in your outlook."

"Did you requisition money?"

"I did add to the cash I had with me when I arrived. We won't have any problems. I have credit cards in my wallet if we run short."

"What is a credit card?"

"It's a plastic card that identifies you and permits a bank to advance money for your purchases. Then the bank sends you an invoice to pay it back."

"How will you pay it back from Hallywalooly?"

"That's a good question. I'm hoping I won't have to

use my credit card except as a payment guaranty when I rent a car and book a hotel room. At payment time I'll use cash."

"That is more complicated than requisitioning things as we do here. I will learn a great deal about Topper life on this assignment."

"Just be sure you don't use the word Topper when we're on the surface. It would not be understood, and it would make you appear unusual. That word is only used in Hallywalooly."

"Agreed. I will follow your lead in anything I say. I sense that Red is here to take us to the best hidden exit for our trip. He is thinking about one that is within walking distance of a car rental firm."

"Sometimes your thought reading capabilities are quite useful. Let's go."

# CHAPTER 22
# – NASA

Mac and Merrilong arrived at NASA's Kennedy Space Center Visitor Complex, parked their rental Buick and started to walk toward the exhibits. As they walked, Mac held Merrilong's hand to give her assurance. When they were about halfway to their destination, he stopped. "I've been thinking. While we're on the surface, I think I should shorten your name to Merri when we speak to people. It's a more normal name here. Would you mind?"

"Merri it is. I want to be as much at home in your world as you are in ours. We may be on a mission, but I am picturing myself as a transplant to this way of life and proving to myself that we would be perfect mates anywhere."

As they neared the exhibits, Merri stopped to take a long look at the Rocket Garden. "Your space ships are so long and thin. They are not at all like those used by the Ancient Ones."

"I grew up hearing stories about people seeing flying saucers. Were the Ancient Ones' spacecraft round and flat?"

"No, they were shaped like our meeting table. That is why I chose that design. They were triangular. They were not nearly as long as those in the Rocket Garden. The circular flying saucers may have been spaceships from one of the visitor groups. There have been other visits to Earth from elsewhere, but they chose to do quick studies of this planet and then move on, while we decided to settle here."

"So flying saucers are real?"

"As real as our rental car."

Mac and Merri mingled with the other tourists and attended most of the major exhibits and demonstrations before they drifted into a group waiting for the next Mission Status Briefing, their ultimate destination.

When the next briefing started, two thirtyish enthusiastic NASA spokespeople approached the podium. They wore standard khaki slacks with dark blue NASA logo T-shirts, introducing themselves as Emma and Ted. Emma started the presentation with a summary of status reports on spacecraft and robotic missions that had already been launched, including the type of data they were sending back and discoveries that NASA scientists had made during their interpretations from the data stream. Then Ted spoke about some of the future missions that NASA planned for the Moon, Mars and beyond. At the end of the presentation, they asked for questions from the audience.

Mac made sure he asked the first question, not knowing how many they would accept. "Ted, I've heard that there are plans for exploration of Titan, one of Saturn's moons. Can you tell us about them?"

"Sure. That's a really interesting destination. Titan has liquid rivers and seas, but the liquid isn't water. The dense opaque atmosphere is mostly methane and nitrogen. The liquid in the rivers, lakes, and streams varies from methane to ethane. Our planned exploration robot is called Dragonfly. It will do flying surveys close to the surface of Titan. Current plans are to launch it in 2027 for arrival at Titan in 2034."

Mac asked his key follow-up question. "How likely is that schedule to be accurate?"

Emma gestured to Ted that she would answer this question. "The dates Ted gave you are planning dates at this time. There are two reasons why they may be delayed or moved up. The first is political. The president at the time of planned launch would have to give this space mission its required priority and the necessary budget to support it. Some presidents are big space enthusiasts and others are not. Sometimes competing national priorities require a reduction in NASA's budget in favor of other programs. We plan based on available technology and time requirements for operations sequencing, but we know there will be outside influences to the timing of our programs. The second reason for possible program changes is competition with alternate technologies. Ted highlighted the flying Dragonfly robot, which is currently planned, but there have been alternate proposals for a robotic submarine exploring the depths of Titan's methane and ethane seas, the largest of which is Kraken Mare. Within the next few years, plans could change to choosing the submarine approach over the flying Dragonfly vehicle. So, in summary, our schedule could slip to a later time frame, but we hope it won't."

Ted and Emma took additional questions, and then the audience started to disperse. Mac and Merri were walking about eight feet away from an older couple when the husband staggered, grabbed his chest, and collapsed. Most people around him stared, not knowing what to do. Merri whispered, "Heal him."

Mac said, "They'll know we're different."

"Do not worry. I'll take care of that."

Mac bent over the collapsed man, whose wife was crying and calling for help. He said, "Here, let me assist you." He placed his left hand on the older man's chest while raising him to his feet with his right hand.

The older man's expression changed from one of severe pain to one of calm serenity. "Thank you. I feel much better now. I don't know what you did, but my pain is gone now."

Mac looked quizzically at Merri. She nodded, squinted, and scanned the crowd around them. Then she took Mac's hand and led him back toward their rental car.

"No one will remember the man's collapse or the way you saved him. I removed several minutes of their memories."

"You constantly amaze me, Merri. You can manipulate the thoughts of others as well as read them."

"Keep this our secret, Mac. I have learned many things in my long life."

"I know you're much older, but to me you'll always be in your early thirties."

"Thanks to our bloodstream exchanges, you will not age either." She kissed him as they approached the car.

In the background they heard a man say, "Newlyweds on their honeymoon. I can always spot them."

# CHAPTER 23
# – REPORT

Jablesh appeared tired and tense as he questioned Mac and Merrilong in their meeting room. "So NASA is definitely planning to explore Saturn's Titan moon?"

Mac nodded. "Going there appears to be definite. How and when they will explore it is subject to some change."

Jablesh tuned into Mac's thoughts. "Exploration by either flying or submarine robots...the submarine would be more dangerous for the descendants of the Ancient Ones there. They have cavern entrances under the surface of Kraken Mare."

Merrilong could not remain silent. "Jablesh, you always have our respect, and we avoid interfering in your affairs whenever possible, but you cannot know about living arrangements on Titan unless you have been in communication with that colony. How do you contact them?"

Mac was sure that Jablesh would react with anger, but, surprisingly, he laughed.

"I should have known that you two would not accept my statements without analyzing the logic behind them. You are individually quite perceptive. As a couple, you are quite astute. My answer to your question, Merrilong, is that When the Ancient Ones departed, they left one of their communication devices behind them. I have guarded it and used it for a very long time, but I have not revealed its existence to others."

Mac said, "Shortly after I arrived in Hallywalooly, I asked Red whether you were in charge of everything here. He replied that you were highly respected because you have been here so long and know the ways of the Ancient Ones. It appears that you know their ways because of this communication device that you have held in secret."

"Mac, Merrilong, please do not think less of me because of this revelation. It is true that my secret gave me an edge over a few other old-timers, but I have made peace with them and discovered that they did not even want the responsibilities I assumed."

Merrilong stood and placed her hands on Mac's shoulders. "I know I speak for both of us in saying that you will continue to have our respect, even without the mystery that shrouded you in the past. We hope that you will allow us to question you on logical details when it becomes important in the future."

Jablesh agreed and suggested that they discuss approaches to handling the Titan problem in the near future. Then he stood and ended the assignment review meeting.

Once Jablesh left, Mac hugged Merrilong. "I'm impressed. You very subtly negotiated our right to question Jablesh's authority whenever he says or does something that is not logical. He's like a poker player who holds his cards close to his vest to avoid revealing anything prematurely. I'll bet he still has secrets that will continue to give him power."

"You are probably correct, but now I want you to teach me this card game called poker. I sense that good poker players are excellent negotiators."

"First, I'll have to requisition or create a deck of playing cards. I should have purchased a deck while we were acting as tourists on the surface. It's time for you to tell me how requisitioning works and what items are available."

# CHAPTER 24
# – MAXINE

In his discussion with Merrilong, Mac learned that he could requisition many useful things in Hallywalooly, but he reached the opinion that they didn't have the variety or specialization of items found in surface world stores. He would go beyond the usual procedures to find what he needed for his plans.

Mac drove his yellow utilizer vehicle to the area where Red normally worked, but found that he was supervising a tunneling project in a remote section of Hallywalooly and would not return for many days. Mac spoke with one of the other Guardians about the temporary cell phone mini-tower that Red had rigged for him when he had telephoned the skydiving group, but none of the Guardians present knew where the equipment was or how to assemble it. Somewhat dejected, Mac drove home.

When he arrived, Merrilong asked whether he had visited the Requisition Center.

Mac took a seat and aired his difficulties. "I'll get to the Requisition Center soon, but I wanted to get a few things that are only available on the surface. Red has a rig that lets me telephone to surface people. I was going to call my old friend, Maxine. Jablesh says she's a Hallywalooly agent. I thought I would ask her to buy my items for me. The problem is that Red is working where I can't reach him, so I'm out of luck as far as contacting Maxine."

"You called Maxine your old friend when you meant old lover. Do not worry about offending me, Mac. We are mates now, and what happened before makes no difference. As you said, she is one of our agents. That means that we have ways of communicating with her. Jablesh usually initiates such contacts, but I am sure the people in our Intelligence Center will comply with my request."

"I didn't know we had an Intelligence Center."

"We must monitor the surface world for news and natural processes that might affect us. Construction projects sometimes trigger the development of sink-holes. Hurricanes can lead to cavern flooding. Information from NASA news releases led to our journey to learn about their programs for Saturn's moon Titan. While the Intelligence Center mostly monitors news passively, it has the capability to send communications to the surface world when required. I will tell them that your need to contact Maxine is in our best interests."

Mac and Merrilong rode the yellow utilizer vehicle through a maze of interconnected tunnels before they reached the Intelligence Center. It had no markings over the narrow entrance and appeared to be a dwelling. Once inside, they were questioned by a receptionist in a small antechamber and then allowed to pass into a much wider chamber where a large staff monitored and recorded data from all regions of Earth plus data streams from satellites and space exploration vehicles.

Merrilong approached the Chief Guardian and explained their request. "We need to contact one of our

Topper agents regarding supplies required for one of our new projects here."

The Chief Guardian, whose name was Hollywing, replied, "In other words, you want this agent to go shopping for you. That is inappropriate, and I will not agree to open the communications channel for you."

Mac saw Merrilong squint at Hollywing. It was the same facial expression she had used at NASA, causing people to lose a few minutes of memory.

Hollywing appeared to be uncertain of herself. Then she said, "Welcome to the Intelligence Center. How may I assist you?"

This time, Mac gestured to Merrilong that he would take the initiative. "I conduct special operations for Jablesh to the surface world. It is imperative that I contact one of our agents there."

Hollywing smiled. "We will be happy to assist. I have heard of your work. You may use the privacy alcove to your right. We have an available disposable cell phone and broadband connection. Your call will not be traceable."

After Merrilong followed Mac into the alcove she said, "You obtained her approval because you are male."

"No, Merrilong, she agreed because I told her things that were true, but that weren't our exact reason for making the call. Toppers call it diplomacy. It isn't always necessary to state exactly why you are doing something."

Mac called Maxine, hoping she would answer the unfamiliar number on her display. When she did, he said, "Hello, stranger. I've heard that you sometimes talk with a man whose name starts with J."

"Hello to you, Mac. It has been a while since we

talked. I've heard that you've moved."

"Yes, I interviewed for the position per your rec-ommendation, and accepted the job offer. Are you still available for support?"

"Of course, Mac, I'll always assist you, even though coupledom is far behind us."

Mac glanced at Merrilong, but saw no change in her expression. Then he gave Maxine a list of supplies that he wanted her to procure."

"Got it, Mac. Don't worry about payment. My under-standing with Mr. J comes with a budget to cover a request such as this. Next time you're in my neighbor-hood, stop in for a visit."

"I'll see if I can arrange a private one sometime. Thanks for helping. Great to hear your voice again."

Merrilong looked question marks at Mac. "I could not understand why you want some of the items on your list."

"They're a mixture of gifts and resource supplies. I feel more comfortable when I have a small bag of tricks handy."

Merrilong repeated her questioning look.

On their way out of the Intelligence Center, Mac thanked Hollywing for her assistance. He expected to need her help again in the future and wanted to main-tain a good rapport with her.

# CHAPTER 25 – PREACHER AND CRUNCH

One week after Mac gave his procurement requests to Maxine, Red arrived with many cartons on his green utilizer vehicle. "I brought these over as soon as they arrived at our surface farmhouse that hides one of our many entrances. They appeared to be important to you."

Mac shook Red's hand as they unloaded the cartons. "Thanks for expediting them. Come on in and rest for a while. You've had a busy schedule lately. I tried to contact you about this procurement, but you were working in a remote location."

"I can use a rest and a root beer if you have one. Now that I am substituting for my old boss, Shorty, I appreciate how much work he did while making it look easy."

Mac set two root beers on the table. "You've done a great job filling in for Shorty."

"I will give myself a passing grade. The longer I work at these projects, the easier it gets."

"On the surface world, we call that the learning curve. The jobs get easier as you become more proficient at doing them."

"It is true. Earlier, I would not allow myself a rest break like this."

"I'm glad you're gaining control over your workload, Red. Later, if Jablesh gives me a suitable assignment, I'd like to invite you to work on it with me. You're a good friend and resourceful worker."

"I would like that, Mac. Now, it is time for me to get back to my current duties. Give Merrilong my greetings."

Red left, and Mac opened the cartons to examine his acquisitions. Satisfied with Maxine's efforts on his behalf, he removed four items and loaded the cartons into a hidden storage niche in the wall. He put two of the four remaining objects in a bag for later use, and left two on the table.

When Merrilong arrived home, she saw Mac sitting by the table smiling at her. "Did something funny happen that you are so cheerful?"

"I'm smiling because I enjoy seeing you and because I have things on the table for you."

"Ah, your purchases arrived." She saw two small boxes on the table. "Am I supposed to open these boxes?"

"You are indeed."

Merrilong opened the smaller box first. "It reads: Playing Cards. We talked about them." Then she opened the second box. "Poker Chips. You are going to teach me to play poker with you. I remember now. I am supposed to hold cards close to my chest so no one can see them. It will be what we do for fun. Will it matter that I can read your thoughts and will know your cards?"

Mac said, "That will make some games more difficult than others. Thanks to our overnight transfusions, I'm beginning to be able to read your thoughts also. We'll have to play variations of poker where we don't know our cards until they are turned over."

"What is in that bag, Mac?"

"Gifts for others."

"I sense you thinking Preacher and Crunch. Are they your friends now?"

"I hope so. I'm going to find them now and give them these things. I'll let you know how they reacted when I return."

Mac expected to find Preacher and Crunch in the cavern that had been set aside for the pilot program on saving endangered species. He knew from his conversation with Red that the holding pens for different kinds of animals were nearing completion. He instructed his utilizer to find the pilot program cavern, and it responded promptly, without extra search time for an unknown destination.

Mac found his two friends building stone walls around a pen, using slabs from a large pile of flat rocks. They looked as though they needed a rest break.

Mac shouted out to them. "Hi, Preacher. Hi, Crunch. Take a break. I brought drinks and some other goodies."

They shook hands and sat on the utilizer cart's deck. Mac handed out fermented root beers. "How long will it be before you start to put animals into these pens?"

Preacher said, "I'm not sure. The wild animals will have to be caught by someone first. They haven't told us whether we're to be catchers or keepers on this project. It'll be too big a job for us to do both."

"Whichever way that decision goes, I have suitable presents for you." Mac opened his bag and handed brown Stetson 3X Beaver cowboy hats to his friends.

Crunch said, "Cool. Don't have to worry 'bout sun down here, but these'll make us feel special."

Preacher laughed. "One of the few times Crunch spoke up before me. He's right, though. Thanks from both of us. Now we'll have to scrounge up some horses to match the hats."

Mac put his empty drink container in the bag that had held the hats. "I don't know whether I can procure horses. You might have to ride zebras from your endangered species collection."

Preacher disagreed. "Putting big Crunch on the back of an endangered animal might kill it. We'll have to keep using our legs. What's happening with you, Mac?"

"I'm expecting some new developments, but I can't give you any specifics yet. I'll let you know if something comes up that can use your talents."

"Good. I'm expecting that Crunch and I will get tired of this animal rescue thing before too long. We do what's asked of us, but don't have the greatest amount of patience. Keep us in mind for anything exciting, Mac."

"I was hoping you'd say that."

# CHAPTER 26 – SINKHOLE

Merrilong met Mac outside their home as he arrived. "Do not come in. Summerly wants to see you at her healer office. I think there is an emergency. I will come along with you.

When they arrived, they saw several utilizer vehicles loaded with supplies preparing to leave. Mac rushed inside and waited as Summerly completed her discussion with one of the Guardians. When she turned toward him, Mac asked, "What's happening? Merrilong suggested it was something serious."

"It is. We had a large sinkhole open up in the area the surface people call Sinkhole Alley. On their maps, it is in Hernando County. I need you to assist me and the other healers there, but first, I want to respray your palms. You will be treating many people who were caught in the rocky debris from the cavern ceiling collapse. I also have to give you more instruction about what you can and cannot do to heal people."

Mac extended his hands, palms up, for the special healing spray. "I didn't realize there were limitations."

"I did not tell you earlier because they did not apply to your immediate assignment. You cannot heal people who have been injured without treatment for more than one day before you get to them, or those who have suffered a heart attack or stroke for more than two hours. You also cannot revive the dead. That is a special procedure that trained Stoppers perform on deceased Toppers who have been designated to become Droppers."

"What about my healing of Preacher and Crunch after they suffered lethal gunshot wounds?"

"Their bodies were still technically alive, and you treated them promptly. Many of those buried by sinkhole debris will not be found within the one day healing period. Do not waste your time and energy on such individuals. Save the ones who were not buried and those who were promptly rescued. That is all you need to know for now. I see Merrilong is with you. She will be able to sense the most viable candidates for healing. Now, go quickly. I will join you as soon as I finish dispensing emergency supplies."

Mac and Merrilong rode the yellow utilizer through the network of tunnels and caverns until it slowed as it neared the collapse site. Mac found a safe alcove for parking, and the two of them ran to the center of rescue operations.

Merrilong spotted a woman sitting on a boulder. She had blood above her ear. "Treat her first, Mac. Her head is bleeding, so it is not a stroke."

Mac ran over to the seated woman. "Sit still, and I'll try to heal your head. It should stop hurting soon." Mac held her head in both hands and felt energy flowing between them.

The woman sat straighter. "Thank you. That feels much better."

When Mac lifted his hands off of her head, the blood

was gone, and there was no sign of an injury. He gestured for Merrilong to lead the woman to a safe area. Then he ran to a Guardian who had fallen from the pile of rocks while trying to pull someone free. "Where are you injured?"

"I think I broke my right leg."

Mac placed both hands on the man's leg and visualized a healthy image of it. After a few seconds he removed his hands.

The Guardian said, "That feels much better. I will be able to return to rescue efforts." He stood, took a couple of steps to test his leg, and then climbed the hill of debris carrying a shovel and a crowbar.

Having seen how Mac had treated his first two patients, several of the Guardians brought injured people to him. They formed a line and waited for Mac to lay his hands on each wounded person in turn. After every treatment, a Guardian escorted the person to an emergency rest area where drinks and food were available. With so many working on rescue efforts, the cavern echoed with shouts and mechanical noises.

As Mac continued his healing work, he noticed a large crowd gathering near the pile of collapsed cave ceiling debris. As it moved around, he caught a glimpse of Summerly and Jablesh with a battered man. Unable to justify leaving his line of healing candidates, he asked Merrilong to find out what was happening in the area with the large crowd.

It took Merrilong several minutes to work her way through the outer rings of the crowd, but when Jablesh spotted her, he requested that people let her approach, and she made rapid progress. Once she reached the center, Merrilong saw Jablesh and Summerly with a rather dazed and bloodied, Topper. Jablesh shouted above the background noise for the crowd to disperse, and they obeyed his command. Then, Merrilong, per Jablesh's request, went to fetch Mac to join them.

When Merrilong and Mac returned, Summerly said, "Mac, you stay here and work with Jablesh. I will perform the few remaining healings."

After Summerly left, Jablesh introduced Mac to the stranger. "This is our newest Topper, Bill Twingberry. He was sleeping in his bed when the sinkhole opened and swallowed half of his house – the half that included his bedroom. Thanks to Summerly's healing efforts, Bill's broken arm, leg, and other injuries are under control, and he has decided to stay with us in Hallywalooly. I would like you to spend some time with him, Mac. You have similar sudden arrival stories."

Mac saw Bill as a middle-aged somewhat sedentary individual who might have an interesting background. "I'll be happy to take him under my wing. Are you a family man, Bill?"

"I had a wife and two sons, but after a bitter divorce battle last year, they moved to the West Coast. I'm on my own now, and apparently starting a new adventure."

Jablesh excused himself and walked away with a frown on his face. This surprised Merrilong, who knew that Jablesh almost never revealed his emotions in his facial expression.

Mac decided he was not quite ready to invite Bill home. Instead, he offered to take Bill on a tour while Merrilong would go home with one of the Guardians. Merrilong's gaze met his, and she nodded her understanding of his thoughts. After Mac and Bill left on the yellow utilizer, she asked a Guardian to take her to the

Intelligence Center. There, she told Hollywing that Mac wanted her to meet him outside the Requisition Center to interview a new Topper arrival.

# CHAPTER 27 – BILL TWINGBERRY

When Mac Blackwell and Bill Twingberry arrived at the Requisition Center after touring the underground gardens, Hollywing was waiting for them. Mac introduced her to Bill as being in charge of orientations for new arrivals. Then, Mac left the two of them and departed for home.

Once they were alone, Hollywing explained the workings of the Requisition Center while reading Bill's thoughts at the same time.

*I didn't fall into a sinkhole. I fell into a gold mine. This really is a separate world from ours. I'll get rich having a ghost writer work with me on a book as soon as I escape this place. Imagine the number of people who will want to know about space aliens living underground.*

Hollywing left Bill to examine computer screen displays of items that could be requisitioned while she contacted Summerly and requested that they meet in the sinkhole cavern.

From the Requisition Center, Hollywing drove Bill past the *Noah's Ark* pilot project and then showed him how all the different caves connected through a network of tunnels that resembled the surface world's highway system. The final tunnel on their tour emerged into the cavern where the sinkhole had collapsed the roof. A large number of Guardians were in the process of retrieving bodies from beneath the rock pile and restoring the chamber to its original emptiness. Summerly awaited them at the spot where she had earlier healed Bill from his injuries.

When Hollywing stopped her utilizer near Summerly, Bill asked, "Why are we meeting with your healer woman?"

Hollywing replied, "You have had your major treatment, but now it is time for Summerly to fine tune the results. Even with two treatments, the process is much shorter than surface hospitalization and medication would be."

Summerly read Hollywing's thoughts and nodded slightly. She asked Bill to sit on the edge of the utilizer platform. Once he had done so, she rested her hands on his head. Within seconds he fell backward and was unconscious. Then she hoisted his legs onto the vehicle's deck and placed her hands at the locations of his original injuries. Bill was restored to the condition he was in after tumbling down the sinkhole.

Hollywing said, "Thank you, Summerly. It is good that I know you can reverse your healings. This man cannot be allowed to survive. He wants to profit in the surface world by revealing our presence underground. We would be invaded if he returned alive to the surface."

"He is now in his original condition after the fall. He will not live long. Once the Guardians have the other bodies removed, the cavern cleaned, and the tunnels ready to seal, have them place Twingberry's body on top of the debris pile and leave that pile a bit unstable. If Toppers climb down to find him, they will see no signs of life or activity in this chamber, and they will not explore the cavern diligently because of the danger of additional rockfalls."

"Good. Our secrets will remain safe. Mac was clever to deliver Bill to me."

# CHAPTER 28 – JABLESH

As they finished breakfast, a new tradition for Merrilong, she stiffened and sat upright. "Jablesh is at our door. He visits frequently. That is unusual."

Mac welcomed Jablesh. "Please join us. Would you like to talk formally in the meeting room, or casually in the kitchen?"

"The kitchen will be fine. I am spending too much time with you and Merrilong to be formal."

When they had settled, Merrilong said, "Try a cup of coffee. It is Mac's favorite morning drink, and I have come to like it too."

Jablesh agreed, but Mac observed that he put his hands on his cup several times, without drinking from it.

"How may we be of service, Jablesh?"

"I am a bit bothered, Mac. Without going into details, I see some difficult times coming for Hallywalooly, and I feel that I will need some additional support. You and Merrilong will be in the best position to assist me, but you will need some confidential training sessions first. Would you agree to that?"

Mac and Merrilong exchanged thoughts. Then Merrilong answered for them both. "We agree."

"I hoped you would. By the way, Mac, I appreciate the way you handled the problem of that man who fell into the sinkhole, Bill Twingberry."

"I decided he needed assessment. Hollywing and Summerly determined what had to be done and carried through with it."

"That shows your abilities to evaluate and delegate. Both of those skills will be needed in the future."

Merrilong said, "You mask your thoughts well, Jablesh, but you are more tense and troubled than normal. Are we approaching a crisis?"

"We may be facing more than one crisis, but not in the immediate future. We will have time to prepare."

Mac stared at him. "Have I been part of that preparation from the time of my arrival?"

"No; you were part of it even before you arrived. Maxine did a good job of determining you were the best candidate for us. She evaluated a few others too."

# CHAPTER 29 – TRUST

After Jablesh left, Mac asked Merrilong, "Do you trust Jablesh?"

"I am not sure I know what you mean by trust. I have known him for a very long time. I know he works for the best outlook for Hallywalooly. Does that cover what you mean?"

"I'm bothered that Jablesh wants us to take on extra responsibilities while he won't share his thoughts with us. He doesn't trust us with his secrets. Why should we do things that might be dangerous without knowing all the circumstances?"

"I see Jablesh keeping information secret because he is the leader. Leaders do not have to reveal all their plans. I see you being bothered by his secrecy because you also have leadership skills. As you gain more responsibility, you will better understand Jablesh's point of view. I am not a leader, so I do not resent his secrets or try to learn more about them. I do not know whether that is trust or not."

"It's either trust or lack of interest. Knowing you as my mate, I'll say it's trust. You're probably right as usual that I'm bothered because Jablesh's secrets potentially interfere with my desire to control my future. Whether

I'm a leader or not, I would like to know what lies before me and control it."

"Did you know the future when you were on the surface world?"

"No, I had to plan based on likelihoods, not knowledge of what was to come."

"Why should it be any different here?"

"Merrilong, you are wise, and I know you are part of my future. I will have to trust Jablesh's intentions, but that won't keep me from probing to find the details of his secrets."

"That is probably a good compromise, Mac. You are always active as opposed to passive when a problem faces you."

# CHAPTER 30 – PREACHER

Preacher climbed down from his stone wall perch as Mac drove up on his utilizer powered cart. "Yo, Mac. Good to see you again. Crunch is off learning about the animals we'll be handling in this pilot project. He's a city boy and only knows about dogs and cats."

"You look good in that cowboy hat I gave you. Changes your whole personality."

"It sure does. I almost greeted you with a 'howdy' instead of a 'yo'. You here for fun or business?"

"Not exactly business, but maybe a favor."

"Always willing to do a favor for a friend. What's up?"

"You've changed a lot since surface world gang days. Are you still willing to bend the rules a bit?"

"That's the kind of stuff makes life, or at least revived life, interesting."

"Here's my problem. I'm doing jobs for Jablesh, but I have no idea where he lives. One of these days, I'll have to find him in a hurry, and I won't know where to look. He keeps his home address secret from just about everyone."

"He is a mysterious dude."

Mac handed Preacher a box. "This box contains a

tracking device and its electronic sensing unit. I know Jablesh comes here periodically to check on the endangered animal pilot project. When he next stops by, clip the tracking device to his robe and then trail him electronically to his home base. Then we'll meet, and you can give me the information.

"That sounds simple enough, so long as I avoid getting caught. That guy is the top dog around here. He could revoke my revival or think up something worse for me. I might need an additional payoff because of the risk."

"Name it, and I'll arrange it if I can."

"I know money doesn't buy stuff down here, but how about arranging for me to have a girlfriend? Hanging with Crunch all the time doesn't cut it."

"All I can say is that I'll try. Merrilong knows more about how things work here than I do."

"Give it your best, Bro, and we have a deal. I'll get word to you when I have something to report."

# CHAPTER 31 – MERRILONG

As they were getting ready for bed, Mac asked Merrilong, "Who assigned you to be my mate?"

"What?"

"When I first went to our old sleeping quarters, you said that you had been assigned to be my mate. Who told you to be with me?"

"I cannot tell you that."

"Why not?"

"You might become unhappy and leave me."

"Don't worry about that. You're the best part of my life right now."

"Only 'right now'?"

"Correction: you're the best part of my life ever."

"Thank you, Mac. In my long life, I have had many mates, but you are the best."

"Merrilong, I think that was a compliment, but you don't have to tell me about your other mates."

"And you do not have to tell me about Maxine."

"Fine. This conversation is getting sidetracked. I originally asked who assigned you to be my mate."

"The answer is that I assigned myself. After Summerly healed you when you first arrived, she contacted me and said that you were very unusual and promising.

She added a few other comments that intrigued me, so I declared my seniority over other possible candidates and assigned myself. I hope you will not now want someone younger."

"You've taught me that age means nothing here because of the unlimited life spans of Stoppers and their mates. I want you."

"Why did you ask the assignment question?"

"I promised that I would try to find a woman for Preacher. He's a Dropper, and I don't know whether Droppers are assigned mates, and if so, from what group."

"Now I understand. At first I felt threatened by your question. Droppers can have mates from any group, but they cannot have children. I happen to know another Dropper who might be good for him. She is dark-skinned and quick-witted."

"Was she chosen as a Dropper because of a particular skill?"

"She was a television weather forecaster, chosen because we may be affected by climate change on the surface world."

"She sounds like a good possibility Merrilong. It'll be interesting to see how she reacts to being matched with a former street gang boss."

# CHAPTER 32
# – TRISHA

Trisha stared at Mac as though he was crazy. "I enjoy spending time with Merrilong, and you appear to be relatively normal, but you want to fix me up with a Dropper who was a street gang leader?"

"Preacher was a gang banger when he was alive, but since he was revived as a Dropper, he's changed. He's easy to get along with now."

"I know about changing after revival. Don't forget, I've been down that road myself. Still, I can't forget that he killed people before he died. He could have been the bastard who shot my cousin Jill when she was sitting on her doorstep. Those gang bangers shoot wild and hit plain folks."

"How would you feel if he were a veteran who killed people during a war?"

"That would be much different. It's not the same."

"Hallywalooly people aren't as aggressive as people on the surface. Just meet with Preacher, and decide for yourself whether he's still dangerous."

"Mac, I don't know you, but I've heard you're one of the good guys. If I meet with him, I won't be doing it for you. It will be because Merrilong has done me more than a few favors. "

"I understand. If I were in your shoes, I'd be extra careful too. We'll go with you to meet Preacher if you wish."

"No way. I'm a big girl now. I'll form my own decision about him. Tell him I'll meet him in the farm cavern at seven tomorrow evening. How will I know him?"

"He's black and he wears a brown cowboy hat."

"That's pretty unique. There can't be two guys like that."

"Actually, that description also fits his friend Crunch."

"I think I prefer someone called Preacher over a guy who calls himself Crunch."

Preacher walked slowly as he passed the rows of plants receiving nourishment from arcs of water spray. Mac had done well to set this meeting up, but now he had to make a good impression. This was new territory for him. When he was alive, he had latched onto relationships with women by demanding them. Preacher knew that he had to earn respect and attention now.

He saw Trisha at the base end of the spray arcs. She was studying the way the fish circulated within their pools. As he approached her, he said, "I don't know why, but watching fish swim usually gives people a peaceful feeling. That's why doctors have them in their lobbies back on the surface. It calms their patients."

Trisha looked up, but she wasn't yet ready to smile. "So you're the big bad gang banger. I'm glad you can carry on a conversation. A lot of the street toughs can't."

"Hello, Trisha; I'm glad I have this chance to meet you. I used to watch you do the weather reports on television."

"When you're on TV, you have no idea how many people are watching or what kinds of problems they have."

"It must be hard, talking to a camera lens without having an audience present to react."

"After a while, it gets to be natural. You see yourself on the monitor and become your own audience. Tell me, why do they call you Preacher? Do you have a religious background?"

"I was religious as a kid, before I got sucked into the gang scene. The preacher label came from my ease with language and talking to the group. They thought I was laying sermons on them, so the nickname naturally followed."

"What do they have you doing down here?"

"That's an interesting question, following the discussion of my name. I'm working on a pilot project for a program to save endangered species of surface animals. My friend Crunch works with me on it. We call our job *Noah's Ark*, so it fits right in with my Preacher label."

Trisha finally smiled. "So two former gang members are working to preserve lives instead of ending them."

"I hadn't thought of it that way. What do they have you doing?"

"I'm supposed to monitor trends and details of climate change in the surface world. It's part of advance planning, but we're just beginning to lay out the procedures for the program."

This time, Preacher smiled. "Don't look now, Trisha, but we're working two ends of the same problem. Climate change is what's responsible for making many animal species endangered. That's why we're trying to preserve enough individuals to keep them breeding."

"When Mac and Merrilong first suggested I meet you, I couldn't think of anything we could possibly have in common. Now, I'm beginning to see potential for our hanging out together."

"Praise the Lord. I thought my future in Hally-walooly would offer nothing but loneliness."

"You have Crunch to keep you company."

"He's a good friend, but not a cure for loneliness. I hope we'll have something work out."

"Slow down, cowboy. Only time will tell how that develops."

# CHAPTER 33
# – REPORT

Merrilong suddenly stopped speaking in the middle of discussing the latest Hallywalooly news and rumors with Mac. She raised her hand in a stop gesture.

Mac stood and stared at her. "What's happening?"

"Preacher is outside our doorway. He is anxious to speak with you. We will resume our discussion later."

Mac went to the front entrance and greeted Preacher. "Merrilong sensed your presence and your need to meet with me. Are you here to let me know about your meeting with Trisha? Will you see her again?"

"No need for doorbells when Stopper sensing talents are handy. Trisha decided to take a chance on me. She didn't exactly say it, but I'm on probation with her to be sure I don't go back to my old surface world ways. That's not why I'm here. I have good news and bad news for you, Mac."

"Start with the good stuff."

"The tracker did its job perfectly. I can lead or direct you to Jablesh's hidden cavern. I never would have found it without the electronic bloodhound unit."

"That's great. Now, what's the bad news?"

"I'm sure Jablesh found the tracking device on his

robe. Right after it arrived at the final destination and stopped moving, its signal disappeared. I think he found the tracking bug and crushed it. I'm sure he won't be happy with either one of us. He'll be sure I planted the bug and tracked him. I'll bet he'll be angry when you show up on his doorstep."

"Don't worry, Preacher. I expected him to know I was there before I arrived. Merrilong detected your arrival here, and Jablesh probably has greater sensing capability than she does. I'm trying to get on an even footing with him. Now I won't have to wait for him to come to me when I need to communicate with him."

"In terms of my gang background, that sounds as though you're planning to make a move on the leader. That could be dangerous, Mac."

"Put it in terms of a pro athlete's bargaining for a better deal. I think I'm here because he needs me for some reason, and I want to get the full story from him."

"That sounds more reasonable. Good luck with that. I'm going to play it cool and lie low. I got to meet Trisha because of this tracking operation. I don't want to lose her because of Jablesh's reaction to it."

"Don't worry. I'll take full responsibility in any confrontation."

# CHAPTER 34 – SECOND SHOE

Merrilong noticed a change in Mac's manner over the next few days. He appeared tense and frustrated. She suggested they visit the Requisition Center to get some unusual items, but his reaction was unexpected.

"Thanks, Merrilong. I know you're trying to cheer me up, but I'd rather wait on that shopping trip until I know what lies ahead of me."

"What lies ahead of you is loving time with me. Is that not enough?"

"I had Preacher track Jablesh to his home cavern. Jablesh discovered the tracking device and smashed it. We have a saying on the surface world about waiting for the second shoe to drop. People always take off two shoes when they go to bed. Jablesh figuratively dropped the first shoe when he smashed the tracking device. I expect him to drop the second shoe by showing anger toward me in some way. I thought he would react right away, but he hasn't. Now, I'm tense because I don't know when he'll take some kind of action."

Merrilong laughed. "You Toppers expect quick responses. Everything has to be fast-paced to fill your limited number of days and years with activity. Stoppers, especially one with Jablesh's many centuries of life, take a longer approach to reactions. You should not be disturbed by the lack of that second shoe falling. By the time he does address the matter, it may have no consequences at all."

"I wish I could share your optimism."

"Jablesh looks favorably on you, for all the tasks you have accomplished since arriving and for future projects he has planned."

"Do you know anything about those planned projects?"

"If I did, you would know too. We are mates, and we share our thoughts better with each passing day. What am I thinking now?"

"You're thinking that you want to go to the Requisition Center and procure some treats that will make me feel better. That cheers me up already. What am I thinking?"

"Yes, we will have sex after we return."

# CHAPTER 35
# – VISIT

After navigating an unmarked path through a maze of tunnels, Mac stood at the entrance to Jablesh's home cavern and waited for permission to enter. It came sooner than expected.

Jablesh emerged from his hallway and gestured for Mac to follow him inside. They passed into a small front chamber where three chairs surrounded a triangular table. Jablesh took a seat at the compact table and signaled Mac to join him. "Your tracking procedure to find my home showed resourcefulness, but why did you not simply ask me where I live?"

"Everyone here treats you with great respect from a distance and refrains from intruding on your personal space. I felt that I would face refusal if I asked for your home's location."

"Well, Mac, you are here now. What do you want to discuss with me?"

"You actively worked to bring me into Hally-walooly, and you have spent a great deal of time educating me to the ways of the Stoppers, as has Merrilong. I have to conclude that you have long-term plans for me that remain hidden at this point."

"I said earlier that I found you to be an astute

thinker. I continue to hold that opinion. I have given you several missions, which you have completed satisfactorily. Your handling of the case of the unacceptable individual who arrived through the sinkhole and your tracking operation to find this place show initiative and resourcefulness. Yes, I have long-term plans for you and your talents, but they are not fully formulated. It would be premature to reveal them now."

"Do these plans include Merrilong?"

"Of course they do, and your nightly transfusion bloodstream exchange will allow them to be long-term from my perspective rather than from your more limited Topper viewpoint."

"Jablesh, you are as close genealogically to the Ancient Ones as anyone in Hallywalooly. Do you feel Earth is your home planet, or do you have greater feelings for the home planet the Ancient Ones left?

"I was born here. You are asking the question that applies to all children of immigrants, whether to a planet or a country. Your family members at some time migrated to your surface world country from another. It is the same thing."

"I have one request for you, Jablesh."

"What is it?"

"Please do not punish Preacher for tracking you on your way home. I take responsibility for asking him to do that. If there are to be any consequences, I should bear them."

"Mac, I applaud your leadership skills. A leader requires supporters. There will be no consequences for your recruiting someone to assist you with a task you deemed necessary. This is all an informal aspect of your training."

"Then, I may return to visit you again?"

"Whenever you feel my input would aid your projects ..."

*That second shoe dropping was quite soft.*

# CHAPTER 36 – REQUISITION CENTER

Mac followed Merrilong into the Requisition Center, expecting to see many counters and shelves displaying goods that were available there. Instead, he found himself facing one of ten large flat-screen displays of categories of goods that were available. Merrilong told him to select any one that looked interesting. He read the listings and announced his selection of *power tools*. A voice responded, "Station Three."

Merrilong led Mac to a row of compact computer screens on a shelf. He stood in front of the one labeled 3, which bore the flashing sign, *power tools, specify type or function*. Mac said, "automated carving tool."

A voice said, "Wood or stone?"

"Wood"

"Size of carving: small, medium, large?"

"Medium"

"Wood block included?"

"Yes"

"Type of wood?"

"Walnut"

"Go to delivery station 3."

Merrilong smiled, "You tried to ask for something that wouldn't be available."

"I've never seen the item I requested. Does it exist?"

"Let's go to the delivery station to find out." She led Mac to a table-height platform at the rear of the chamber.

Mac stared in disbelief. On the platform was a machine tool with a computer screen plus a one foot square by two feet long block of walnut wood. "These look like the items I requested. Will the machine actually produce any carving I wish?"

"Input a drawing or a photograph, and you will find out."

"Thank you Merrilong. I will have fun testing this when we get home. I'm only now beginning to realize how much technology there is in Hallywalooly. I will have to meet the technical people."

"You have already met one of them – me."

Mac realized that he had a lot more to learn about Merrilong. "Did you design this amazing system?"

"It was long ago, and I was one member of the team that created it. Stopper technology had a big head start on that of surface world Earth."

As they left with Mac's new treasures, they saw Trisha and Preacher approaching.

Mac placed his packages on the ground. "Hello, you two. This is an amazing place. You can get almost anything you want."

Trisha nodded. "I've shopped here before. It's something else. We're getting a couple of pieces of furniture today. I decided to let this bad boy move in with me on a trial basis."

Preacher said, "I don't know if I'll ever clear my reputation, but I've cleaned up my act. I'm a helper now."

Trisha said, "We'll see how good a helper you are. After we finish shopping, I'll wear your cowboy hat so it doesn't get in your way while you're carrying furniture."

"That furniture will be easy for me. It marks a trip to the Promised Land. I couldn't stand rooming with Crunch any longer. He snores like mad."

Trisha smiled. "How do you know I don't?"

# CHAPTER 37 – SCULPTURE

Once home, Mac set his automated carving machine and walnut wood block on the meeting table for examination. Merrilong joined him.

"Mac, why are you staring so thoughtfully at the machine? It will function properly. We can test it together."

"It's amazing technology, to be able to create anything you need upon command. I'm also awed that you were on the team that built the system that generates such products."

"The original systems were developed when the Ancient Ones left their home planet to look for new home worlds. You never know in advance what you will need on another planet, and you cannot carry every possible thing with you, so you need to be able to construct almost anything at your destination. It is similar to what NASA is doing right now. They will carry three dimensional printers to the moon and Mars in order to build housing shelters from materials they find at their destinations."

"Merrilong, are you saying you are one of the Ancient Ones and that you were alive when they first traveled?"

"Of course not, Mac; their technology was developed long before my birth. I simply worked on the much more recent system that is in the Requisition Center. Does that ease your mind?"

"Yes, but that still means that you are a super special smart individual."

"Mac, I thought you knew that already. Is that not why you are happy to be my mate?"

"I'm learning more reasons every day."

"Good. You continue to impress me too. No one has ever before insisted on being equal to Jablesh, and he has accepted your leadership qualities."

"Enough mutual admiration. How do I make this machine work?"

"You feed it a drawing or a photograph of the object you want, and it will carve a sculpture of that item from the block of wood."

"The machine doesn't have a power cord, and I don't see any sockets in our walls for electric power."

"Mac, you do not need those things here. We radiate power into our machines from power sources built into the cavern walls. You have photographs in your cell telephone. Select one; hold the phone up facing the machine; and say *Create*."

Mac mounted the walnut block on the input platform. He chose a photograph of him approaching the ground on a parachute that had been taken and shared by one of the instructors. As directed, he held it up facing the machine and said, "Create."

The carving machine activated, and the block of wood fed slowly into the internal mechanism. The production process was surprisingly quiet, and the display screen showed the increasing percentage of completion. When the screen showed 100%, a caption appeared: *Finished object will emerge in two minutes.*

Mac waited. Two minutes later, a panel door opened revealing the completed sculpture. "I can't believe this. The machine made a three-dimensional carving from my two-dimensional photo, and it painted it too. It even has a base to support the statue of me and my parachute as we're barely off the ground."

Merrilong patted his shoulder. "You showed the machine a colored picture, including the ground below your feet, so it matched what it saw. What will you do with the statue?"

"Give it to you, of course. I hope you like it."

"Thank you, Mac. I will keep it in a favorite place always, as a reminder of how you dropped into my life from above."

"And every time I look at it, I'll think of your many hidden talents, including some that I have not yet discovered."

# CHAPTER 38 – ANIMALS

Mac looked over at Merrilong as they ate breakfast. "I have a question about something that has been bothering me."

"What is it?"

"When Jablesh first told me about Stoppers being able to read another person's thoughts, he said they could only sense thoughts during a crisis. I'm getting that talent from you due to our nightly bloodstream exchanges, and right now I sense Preacher outside our door waiting for me to come out. There's no crisis."

Merrilong said, "Do not tell Jablesh, but I have greater sensitivities than most other Stoppers, and because I have them, you are developing them too. Now go outside and greet your friend. He has news for you."

Mac stepped out of his doorway and waved to Preacher. "Hi. Do you want to come in for coffee or that spiked root beer?"

"Not today, Mac. It's a milestone for our Noah's Ark pilot project. We get our first critically endangered animals today, and we'll soon know whether our training pays off. They're arriving by boat in a hidden Atlantic Ocean cave near our new animal sanctuary. I've seen these big animals in zoos, but Shorty thinks we'll be able to handle them by putting them behind stone walls and in chambers with narrow entrances. I hope he's right."

"What animals are coming?"

Preacher looked at his list. "It says here that we'll be getting pairs of Black Rhinos, Orangutans, Sumatran Elephants, and Sunda Tigers. This will be a challenge."

"Good luck to you. I hope it goes well. You have a big job ahead of you."

Preacher left on his construction-rugged utilizer, and Mac went inside to relay the news to Merrilong. "The Noah's Ark pilot project is starting out with some of the most difficult animals on Earth arriving today. We'll soon know whether this was a practical idea."

"You sound doubtful."

"Learning how to control and take care of any one of these animals would be a major task. We're starting with four pairs of totally different critically endangered animals. I'll go over later to see if they need extra help."

Mac headed for the animal rescue pilot project after he requisitioned another block of hardwood and had his carving machine make a sculpture of Merrilong from a photo he took with his cell phone's camera. Now she had one of him on his parachute and he had one of her laughing. He found her attractive for many reasons, but perhaps the most special was the way she looked when she laughed.

As he approached the animal sanctuary, Mac saw two Guardians blocking the tunnel entrance and waving at him to stop. He halted his utilizer and walked over to them. "Is there a problem?"

"The orangutans and the tigers are loose. Our enclosure designs made it too easy for them to climb the rocks and escape. Preacher, Crunch, and their assistants are trying to herd the animals back into their walled pens, but they have not yet been successful."

"I came over to assist them, but I don't think they have the right tools for rounding up loose animals. I'm going to get some supplies, and then I'll be back to help."

Mac drove his utilizer to the Requisition Center. There, he selected *Gardening* as his main category because there was no listing for *Animal Control*. Once assigned to work station number 5, he asked for "Telescoping tube, metal, hook on end, quantity four".

"Extended length?"

"Sixteen feet"

"Number of sections?"

"Four"

"Hook facing upward or downward?"

"Upward"

"Next Item?"

"Heavy rope weighted net, quantity four."

"Shape?"

"Square"

"Side length?"

"Twelve feet"

"Location of weights?"

"weights on edges"

"Next item?"

"Tranquilizer dart rifle"

"For small, medium, or large animal?"

"Large"

"Quantity of darts?"

"Twelve"

"Next Item?"

"Order complete."

"Proceed to delivery station."

Mac loaded his purchases on his utilizer vehicle and returned to the entrance to the animal sanctuary. Seeing his load of supplies, the Guardians waved him through the tunnel to the active area.

Mac emerged from the tunnel to a scene of complete chaos. Animal roaring, trumpeting and screeching echoed from the rock walls. A tiger stood on top of a tall pile of rocks roaring at an orangutan sitting on a still higher rock perch. Guardians were climbing toward the animals carrying clubs and shouting.

Preacher and Crunch ran over to Mac's powered cart, obviously confused as to what to do next. Preacher said, "We weren't prepared for this. In addition to this standoff between this tiger and orangutan, their mates are hiding somewhere in the cavern, but we haven't located them. At least the elephants and rhinos are only making noise so far."

"I have a tranquilizer rifle with twelve darts. I hope your aim will be good, so that we don't have too many misfires. We should tranquilize the animals up high on the rocks. Then we can use the telescoping poles to get the nets over them and drag them down. Depending on their locations, we may be able to drop nets over the other animals without tranquilizing them. Once we get them all back in their pens, we can rig the nets above the pens so they don't climb out again."

Crunch said, "Good thinking, Mac. I'll take the rifle. The Guardians will be better than us at using the poles and nets."

Preacher just nodded, amused by Crunch's volunteering to lead the charge.

As Crunch climbed the rock pile, the Guardians

moved in closer to watch, and the tiger changed his focus from the orangutan to Crunch, snarling and pawing the air in his direction. Crunch found a ledge halfway up where he could shift to his right to aim at the tiger's shoulder. Steadying himself against a large boulder, he fired.

The tiger, startled by the dart in his shoulder, turned his head to try to bite at it. Then, the tranquilizer started to take effect, and he lost his footing, tumbling downward toward his antagonist, but getting wedged on rocks three feet above Crunch's head. There, he completely lost consciousness. Unphased, Crunch aimed his rifle at the orangutan, but missed on the first shot when the simian swung to a different perch. His second shot found the orangutan's hind quarters as the animal reached the peak of the rock pile. There it collapsed.

Crunch climbed down to the ground and shouldered his rifle. "Now I'm off to find the other orangutan and tiger. The Guardians can pull these two down."

Preacher shook his head. "You're pretty cool, man, but I'd be picking up pieces of you if that tiger had fallen all the way down and taken you with him."

"I felt safer than I did on city streets when we were alive and gang banging."

Preacher nodded. "There's something to be said for that. Mac, you stay here and supervise the Guardians. They'll be using your nets and poles, so you probably want to see how well they work. I'll go with Crunch. We were pretty good at spotting street danger, so hopefully that will help with sneaking up on wild animals."

Preacher and Crunch went into hunting mode, moving as quietly as possible among the walled pens. After they had searched for about five minutes,

Preacher held up his hand in a *stop* gesture. Without saying a word, he pointed toward the entrance to the elephant enclosure, where he had heard the huge beasts stomping their feet restlessly. They peered over the wall and spotted the remaining tiger high on a cliff ledge preparing to jump on an elephant's back.

Crunch took aim and pulled the trigger. The tranquilizer dart struck the tiger in her right front leg as she leaped toward the elephant. The tiger fell short of her mark onto the ground, not quite tranquilized because she was hit in a limb instead of her body.

Both elephants reacted, goring the intruder with their tusks and stomping on her with their massive feet. When they finished and backed away, the tiger was a bloody carcass, if not dead, very close to it.

Preacher scratched his head. "I think we flunked the zookeeper test. Crunch, you go hunt the missing orangutan, while I get the Guardians and their nets."

When Preacher told Mac about the encounter, Mac said, "Take a couple of the Guardians and their nets and pull that female tiger out of the elephant pen. If possible, get her back to her own pen, but keep her under the net. As a healer's assistant, I'll try to revive her, but not unless she's restrained by the weighted net."

"I don't blame you at all for being cautious with that monster. We'll see if we can even move her all the way back to her pen."

The elephants settled down when their tiger enemy was finally dragged out of their enclosure. Then they kicked dirt over the bloody spot where the tiger had been.

A half hour later, Mac entered the tiger pen and found the Guardians resting after their ordeal of dragging the female tiger's carcass back. They stood as he arrived.

"You did a great job to get her back here. Now, tie the net so that she can't attack while I try to revive her."

The Guardians and Preacher drove stakes into the rock floor and tied the weighted net to them.

Mac had no idea whether his healing skills would work for animals as well as people, but he was determined to do his best to save this beautiful but savage creature. He reached through the net and rested his hands on the tiger's head. There was no immediate response. Then he rested one hand on the head and the other on the shoulder of the beast. He thought he felt a tremor in the animal's body. A few minutes later, he saw that open cuts and gashes were closing. After about ten minutes, the tiger rose to her feet. The net restrained her from large movements or attacks, but after a brief stretch, the creature was content to sit and rest quietly. It wasn't clear whether the healing process or her severe injuries had left her docile and subdued.

In the distance, they heard Crunch calling. "Where is everyone? I have a tranquilized orangutan that needs a ride back to her pen."

# CHAPTER 39 – RECOMMEN- DATION

Mac waited outside the entrance to Jablesh's home, knowing that his presence would soon be sensed. Mac was pleased to realize that his own sensitivities had increased to the point that he knew Jablesh was at home before that leader reacted to his presence.

The brown-robed figure appeared in the entrance and beckoned for Mac to join him inside. Once inside, Mac was surprised to see two cups of coffee on the small triangular table.

"You either anticipated my arrival, Jablesh, or you brew coffee very quickly."

"A little of both. I did sense your intention to visit before you arrived, and I quickly reheated coffee left over from yesterday. I hope you don't mind that it's not freshly brewed. I don't bother with cooking very much."

"The reheated drink is fine with me. The surprise is that you are a coffee drinker. Coffee is a surface world habit."

"I heard that you had problems at the pilot animal sanctuary project yesterday."

"It got pretty ugly, and we almost lost a few endangered animals. Fortunately, my healing skills apparently work with animals as well as people. I managed to revive a Sunda Tiger that the elephants badly gored and stomped after she tried to attack them."

"We knew there might be learning problems connected with keeping these animals in Hallywalooly."

"It's more than a matter of learning how to care for them. Many of these endangered animals are natural enemies. Whenever they get the chance they'll attack each other. The same applies to endangered insects, birds, fish, and aquatic mammals."

"This is only a pilot program, Mac. I'm sure we will learn how to better house and control these creatures."

"That's partly my point. You have suggested a very worthwhile program, but it's too big. We're having troubles with the pilot effort after introducing only eight animals. Consider the scope of efforts all over the planet with all types of creatures. They have to be safely quartered, fed, kept in compatible habitats, and in some cases moved over long distances; all this while you are trying to keep the Toppers from realizing that Hallywalooly and other Stopper outposts exist. I don't think it's the best approach."

"Aha! Your last comment suggests that you have a better way of rescuing endangered species."

"I recommend that we let NASA take the lead on this project. I've learned that some of their people are pushing a much simpler idea. They want to gather, not the creatures, but samples of their DNA. They would store this bank of DNA on Earth's moon, where it would be safe from climate change, damage associated with warfare, and other hazards. When needed at some future time, they would retrieve appropriate DNA samples and clone new creatures via the bodies of their closest living relatives. They've already done successful cloning experiments to save the black-footed ferret and a few other creatures."

"Do you think NASA will make this a full-fledged and funded project?"

"You've said that agents from Hallywalooly have successfully encouraged desired surface world behaviors in the past. It would be much easier for us to covertly encourage this project than to capture and control endangered creatures on a global scale."

"If I approve your recommendation, what do we do with the animals we already have and the people assigned to the existing project?"

"We can protect the few animals we now have by using surface agents to offer them to zoos. Endangered pairs of animals would be welcomed with very few questions asked. It would simply take a touch of diplomacy. The zoos could be told the creatures are a gift from the countries where they are native in the wild. I'm sure we can find other worthwhile projects for the people involved. While we develop new programs, they can work on refurbishing the animal sanctuary for people to live there. Others could be involved in missions to encourage NASA regarding the moon-stored DNA project."

"Alright, Mac, you have made good points. We will accept your recommendation. I will notify all those assigned to the animal sanctuary project of the change and their future responsibilities."

Mac left Jablesh's home feeling much better about the future.

Jablesh watched him depart. *His leadership potential is being realized. Soon, he will be ready for advanced training.*

# CHAPTER 40 – RED

One morning, when Mac and Merrilong returned from obtaining vegetables from the gardens, they saw Red waiting for them outside their home.

Mac parked his utilizer vehicle next his visitor's. "Hello, Red, I hope you haven't been waiting long."

"Not too long, and it gave me a chance to think. I'm usually too active to simply sit and relax."

Merrilong said, "There is no need to stay out here. Would you like to come inside for drinks or to sit and be comfortable?"

"That would be fine. I am here to talk with Mac, but please join us if you wish."

"You two sit and talk in the meeting room. I will bring drinks and join you in a few minutes."

Once they had settled at the big triangular table, Mac asked, "What can I do for you, Red?"

"Ah, you have not heard. The proper topic is what I can do for you. I am here to give you advance notice. Jablesh says that after we finish reworking the animal sanctuary area for people to live there, I will be assigned to be your assistant. Apparently, he feels you will need one."

Merrilong heard Red's revelation as she returned with a tray full of drinks. "Jablesh is testing you, Mac. He wants to know whether you will feel comfortable planning projects and delegating authority to others to help run them."

"That's very subtle. Instead of asking me to do something directly, he's looking to discover what I'll do on my own."

Red agreed. "Jablesh likes to lead without making it obvious that he is doing so."

Mac thought for a moment. "Red, do you have experience on the surface world?"

"Yes, I have spent time there, making repairs following hurricane damage. At such times people accept help from anyone who arrives on the scene, without asking questions."

"Can you drive a truck on surface roads?"

"I have driven a few, but I do not have what they call a license."

"Go to the Intelligence Center, and tell Hollywing that you need a Florida truck driver's license. It should say that you can drive large trucks as well as small ones. She will know how to counterfeit that document for you."

"Mac, having the document is fine, but will I have a large truck for practice of my driving skills?"

"You will have plenty of time to practice. Is there an opening from Hallywalooly to the surface with a ramp that a truck can descend and climb again?"

"There is not one now, but we can build one for temporary use and then close it up after we finish using it if it is no longer needed."

"Good. The surface end of the ramp would have to be hidden somehow."

Merrilong said, "I think we once built an exit that came up inside an abandoned commercial garage building. We could do the same thing with a ramped drive-way. Perhaps the same building would be available, Red."

"I will check on that. An entrance inside a building with garage doors would be perfect. When must this entrance be ready?"

Mac put his cell phone on the table. "First, you will have to set up that miniature tower that will enable me to make telephone calls to the surface. I would plan on a period of about one month before you will be driving a truck to the surface."

# CHAPTER 41
# – MAXINE

"Hello, Mac; what inspired you to call me today? Perhaps I should have answered with a 'Howdy' after purchasing those cowboy hats for you."

"Maxine, I see I'm still in your contact list if my name came up on your display. Those hats were for two friends of mine. This time, I'm going to ask you for a couple of more complex favors. I hope you won't mind."

"Mac, you're the one source of adventure in my current life. Ask away."

"This could require assistance from your husband too. Would he be willing to get involved?"

"This sounds interesting. He trusts me and will go along with whatever story I spin for him."

"Good. Here's the scoop. We tried a pilot project aimed at warehousing endangered animals here, and it didn't work out well. I'll need you to rent a couple of suitable trucks for our use in moving them. Then, we'd hope your husband would use his status as a bank vice president to act as our broker to convince one or more zoos to accept our animals."

"Were they stolen, or illegally obtained?"

"No, we procured them through wildlife preservation groups based on our pledge to care for them in an animal sanctuary."

"You simply failed to give them the location of your sanctuary."

"You guessed it, Maxine. Now it's time to enrich the collection of a zoo, perhaps more than one."

"How many animals and what types?"

"We're looking for homes for eight animals, one male/female pair each of Black Rhinos, Orangutans, Sumatran Elephants, and Sunda Tigers."

"Wow! You don't do anything small. I'll tell Charles, my husband, that this will be an anonymous donation from an animal sanctuary that does not want to be identified. Any zoo should jump at the chance to get breeding pairs of these rare creatures."

"Our only stipulation will be that the accepting zoo or zoos must avoid publicizing the transaction. We won't want investigative reporters trying to discover the source of the animals."

"Understood, Mac. I think the zoos would want to keep things quiet so that animal cruelty groups wouldn't have any ammunition for conspiracy stories."

"Thanks, Maxine. I knew I could depend on you."

"You could have depended on me even more if your business hadn't gone broke. We were a good couple once."

"The best, but you're not implying that you married Charles Barkson for his money, are you?"

"Hell, no! He's the best thing that ever happened to me, but a girl can still fantasize about what might have been."

"Fair enough. You're still my most dependable friend."

"I guess I'll have to settle for that. Call me again next

week, and I'll give you information about rental trucks for transporting large animals. They'll be big and special. Zoo negotiations will take a lot longer."

"We have one to two months to make that happen. If it takes much longer, we may have to return the animals to their original geographically-distant sources."

"Understood. I'll start discussing the project with Charles tonight."

"Wonderful, Maxine; you're the greatest."

# CHAPTER 42 – PREACHER AND TRISHA

When Mac visited the cavern side-chamber where Preacher and Trisha had moved in together, he found a very surface world device – a doorbell. Then he realized that a Dropper couple needed a means of knowing when they had a visitor. They couldn't simply sense a person's presence as could Stoppers and their transfused Topper mates. He pushed the button and heard the chime echoing off rock walls inside.

A minute or so later, Preacher emerged; bare-chested, unbuttoned shirt hanging loosely over his jeans, but crowned with his brown Stetson hat.

"Greetings, Mac; what brings you to our corner of Hallywalooly?"

"I wanted to give you the latest update on Noah's Ark."

"Rumor has it that the pilot project got cancelled after we had tigers and orangutans running loose."

"That incident showed us how difficult it would be to build animal sanctuaries in underground caverns all over the world for animals that were mortal enemies to each other. So, you're right. It's cancelled."

"Are you here to relay Jablesh's new assignment for me?"

"Yes, it's a new project. No, it's from me, not Jablesh. He gave me responsibility to tie up all the loose ends from the animal project, and I'll need your help."

"That sounds cool. I'm more at ease with you than the old man in the brown robe. By the way, I'd invite you in, but Trisha is still sleeping."

"That's par for an unannounced visit. Here's the deal. I'm working on arranging for one or more zoos to take our animals. Red is training to drive special trucks that will hold them, one pair at a time. We'll have a special ramped entrance for the truck by the time we're set with the zoos. Then I'd like you and Crunch to be the animal wranglers, while Red sticks to the driving chores. I'll also ask you to be the primary spokesman in dealing with zoo people. Red is not experienced with surface world matters. How does that sound?"

"I'm good with that plan. Crunch has been lost without a job or a woman, so he'll be fine too. I'll fix it with him. Can I take Trisha?"

"Not this time, Preacher. She's too easily recognized from all her time on television. I'll try to set up something that includes her in the future."

"Mac, I get vibes that you're the new boss here. Did I miss something?"

"Frankly, I don't know what my job is. Jablesh tells me to take care of something, and I figure out how to get it done."

"Then he's still in charge?"

"Absolutely. I still have lots to learn about Hally-walooly. If you'd rather not be part of my work team, let me know."

"I'm in. You keep things interesting, and you set me up with Trisha, so I owe you big."

"Once we get past the animal relocations, we'll do something together, you and Trisha plus me and Merrilong. Hallywalooly needs more socializing."

"Watch out, Mac. Jablesh won't sign off on that."

# CHAPTER 43 – MOVING DAY

Seven and a half weeks later, Hallywalooly had a wide, blacktopped ramp leading to a surface warehouse with oversized garage doors. Red had practiced many times driving the huge truck he called the Elephant and Rhino Wagon plus a slightly smaller one suitable for tigers or orangutans. For the previous two weeks, each animal had eaten its food out of its travel crate to increase its comfort with new, confined surroundings. By moving day, all the animals were comfortable with Preacher, Crunch, and their assistants passing close to them, delivering their food, and refreshing the straw on the floor of their crates.

Immediately before sealing each animal within its ventilated crate, Summerly, the healer, touched it gently to calm it and eliminate travel trauma.

The negotiations with zoos had resulted in an arrangement that all the animals would be delivered to a single easily accessible zoo which would keep one pair and then transfer the other three pairs to other zoos. The primary facility would have first choice of the species it wanted to retain in compensation for its expediting transfers of the remaining animals to the other three zoos. This was satisfactory for all concerned. The crew from Hallywalooly delivered animals to a single location. The primary zoo had the opportunity to examine all the animals and select the ones they wanted. Equally important, limiting each of four zoos to one new pair of endangered animals would minimize publicity as compared with one zoo receiving all four breeding pairs.

Red drove to the animal pens in the smaller of the two trucks for his first load. They would take the orangutans first, as the least likely to cause trouble. Guardians loaded the two individual crates through the rear doors of the cargo trailer using a compact construction crane. Drivers alongside the truck on highways would not realize its cargo was live animals.

Once their load was secured from shifting during the trip, Preacher and Crunch joined Red in the truck cab. As they drove up the ramp, Crunch opened the remote-controlled garage door that concealed the Hallywalooly ramp from anyone who entered the warehouse. That building was more than large enough for Red to swing the truck in line with the exit garage door leading to the surface road. Crunch used his second remote control to open the exit door and then close it behind them as they drove away.

The one-hour trip to the primary zoo was uneventful except for periodic thumps as the orangutans climbed and jumped between bars mounted to the sides of their crates. When they arrived at the zoo, they were directed to a service entrance away from public view at the rear of the property. Red drove through the entrance, and a zookeeper, upon learning their cargo was orangutans, directed them to a loading dock at the rear of the primates building. Red backed the truck to the dock and turned off the engine. Preacher and Crunch entered the building to deal with the zookeepers there. Preacher noticed that the thumps made by the crated animals became more frequent after the truck stopped. They also started vocalizing in response to zoo animal noises, their calls sounding like a tentative dog bark with a trailing lilt.

After shaking hands with the nearest zookeeper, Preacher said, "The orangutans are getting more animated now. They'll need to calm down before you open their crates."

She nodded her agreement. "Glad to see you're concerned for their welfare. Sometimes we receive animals from people or groups that treat animals like objects. By the way, I'm Matti, short for Matilda, a name that's too old-fashioned for me."

"I go by Preacher, and my over-sized partner is Crunch."

"He appears to be capable of handling almost any animal."

"You should have seen him handle a tranquilizer rifle when two tigers got loose ... Crunch, come over here and meet Matti."

"Hi; I was listening to the calls and growls from some of your other animals. Can't see them from here, but they sound active."

"Glad to meet you, Crunch. Our creatures act up when they hear or smell new animals."

Preacher said, "Matti, if you think they're active now, wait 'til we get back on our other trips. We're bringing tigers, rhinos, and elephants. We'd better get going before our driver gets antsy. We have to do three more trips today. Have your people ready to receive big cats next."

Preacher and Crunch returned to the truck, and Red started it moving as soon as they shut the cab door. "With our schedule, we cannot spend much time socializing."

When Red backed the truck down the ramp from the warehouse, other Guardians had already raised the first tiger crate on the crane for loading. Twenty minutes later, the truck with two tiger crates hidden inside its trailer was headed back up the ramp to the warehouse and the road beyond.

As they approached the zoo for the second time, Red said, "This is the last of the easy trips. The monster flatbed truck with rhinos and elephants will be much harder."

Matti and her zookeeper crew were well-prepared for the arrival of the tigers, but the big cats weren't feeling friendly as the unloading began. She called out above their snarling to her associates, "We'd better keep this pair in the isolation cage until we decide which animals we're keeping here. They might try to attack our resident cats if we mingle them right away."

This time, Preacher and Crunch did little more than wave after unloading was complete. They knew transporting the remaining animals would be a major challenge.

When they returned to the warehouse that hid the ramp, Red parked the truck with the enclosed trailer, and started the engine on a bigger truck with a long flatbed trailer that was parked at the far end of the building. Although he had practiced driving this unit over several days, he had to change his driving habits as he tackled the bigger rig. Red's shirt was wet with sweat by the time the flatbed was in loading position at the bottom of the ramp. The larger crates for the Black Rhinos were matched for handling with a larger crane than had been used on the previous two trips. Because of the length of the flatbed trailer, loading was complicated by its being on an uphill slant as it was loaded. The lack of sides on the trailer helped as the smelly rhino crates were lifted to their target positions and then lowered onto the trailer deck. As soon as each crate met the deck, a crew of Guardians secured it in place with straps and motion-limiting pins. Once he was satisfied that the crated live load would not shift, the crew chief signaled Red to start his engine and depart.

As they started up, Preacher said, "I hope this thing has enough power to get us up that ramp. I wouldn't look forward to having to push it."

With its heavy load, the truck inched up the ramp and then turned and backed several times within the warehouse before it was lined up with the exit door. Once finally on the road, they found the biggest hazard was traffic slowing alongside them to stare at the huge animals through gaps between the boards of the crate. The distance to the zoo was the same as on the previous trips, but this time it seemed a lot longer due to their need to drive more slowly while monitoring the animals' condition.

When they reached the zoo, Matti directed them to a flat area rather than the loading dock. There, after removing all the security pins and straps, a large crane raised each crate off the flatbed trailer and pivoted to lower it to the ground next to the truck. They took a break for some cool drinks before tackling the final trip with the elephants. During this break, Preacher noticed normally quiet Crunch talking at lengthy with Matti and several of the other zookeepers.

Red soon fired up the truck engine, signaling that it was time to leave. When Preacher and Crunch climbed back into the truck cab, Crunch returned to being his usual silent self. Preacher decided not to question him in case Crunch was in one of his foul moods.

By the time the elephants in their crates were loaded on the flatbed truck and secured in place, it was already twilight. While Red knew the zoo people would wait for them, regardless of schedule, he was concerned about whether the crates would be too high to pass under the exit door of the warehouse and one highway bridge that had slightly lower clearance than the others. During his time of training as a truck driver, Red had voiced his concerns about load clearance to Mac, who responded by supplying Red with an extra piece of equipment he had requisitioned.

The truck climbed the ramp slowly, due to the incline and its heavy load. When it reached the top, it barely cleared the warehouse ramp-concealing door opening. Once inside the warehouse, Red maneuvered several times to be sure the vehicle would be straight as it approached the exit door. Crunch pressed the remote button to raise the door. When it was fully open, they saw that the downward curving bottom panel would not quite clear the tops of the elephant crates. They had anticipated this possibility and had stored a tall ladder and two coils of stout rope in the warehouse to handle it.

Crunch climbed the ladder with a coil of rope over his shoulder. He passed the rope over a ceiling truss and tied it to a cleat on the bottom of the downward curving panel. Then he climbed down, cleared the ladder out of the way, and motioned for Preacher to join him. Together, they pulled the rope to hoist the downward curving panel back against its spring, so that it became horizontal. While they held the door in this position, Red slowly drove the truck underneath it and out to the long driveway. Then Crunch and Preacher released the rope, untied it from the cleat, and pulled it down for storage. First obstacle overcome.

Once on the road, they traveled in the slow lane, knowing the heavy truck could not quickly change lanes and avoid other vehicles. Progress was steady. Other vehicles slowed down to survey the huge crates but then accelerated and passed the truck. As they approached the overpass that might not have enough clearance, Red slowed down and triggered his emergency flashers. They came to a full stop ten feet from the overpass.

Preacher and Crunch got out of the truck cab. Preacher stood at the rear with a red flag, waving traffic around them, while Crunch climbed up onto the flatbed trailer to judge whether they had enough clearance. After taking a series of views from various angles, he announced. "We miss clearing it by about two inches."

Red climbed down from the driver's seat. "Here's the plan. We will have to let some air out of all the tires until we drop down low enough to clear the overpass."

Preacher asked, "Will our remaining tire pressure be high enough to drive our elephants the rest of the way?"

"Decreasing air pressure is the first part of the plan. After we drive under the overpass, we uncover the object under the tarp between the crates. Mac supplied us with a heavy-duty battery-powered air compressor. This operation will take some time, and we will have to dodge some traffic, but it should work."

Slightly less than one hour of steady activity later, they were on the other side of the overpass and ready to roll again. Tired and dirty, they reached the zoo maintenance entrance well after the sun had set, but the staff had floodlights illuminating the unloading area with the construction crane. Exhausted, Red, Preacher, and Crunch went for drinks while the zookeepers handled removal of the elephant crates from the flatbed trailer.

After their rest break, Red and Preacher returned to the unloading area in time to see the elephants being led out of their opened crates into a fenced temporary enclosure.

Matti walked up to them. "Those are magnificent creatures. I'll vote for keeping them here and letting the other zoos share the orangutans, tigers, and rhinos."

Preacher said, "They're all pretty rare. I think I'll miss working with them."

"I understand you had some problems on the road."

"Nothing we couldn't handle. Red and our boss planned it out well. Did you get that road problems story from Crunch, Matti?"

"I did, and that brings me to our next topic. Crunch wants to stay here and work at our zoo. A big guy like him would be a great addition to our staff. He told me to tell you he won't be going back with you."

Red started to object, but Preacher interrupted. "I guess he got even closer to these animals than I did. He seems to be hiding so that I can't talk him out of his choice. Tell him it's good with us, but our boss may want to come and discuss his future with him."

Red started to object again, "But …"

"No more time for talking, Red. It's late, and everyone wants to go home and get some sleep. Let's head for the truck." Preacher gave Red a look that ended his attempts to keep Crunch from staying.

When they climbed back into the big truck, Red said, "Are you crazy, Preacher? Jablesh will not be at all happy about a Dropper leaving Hallywalooly and living on the surface."

"You're probably right, but if we make a stink about it now, they'll know there's something unusual about Crunch, and they might even refuse to keep the animals. Would you want to have to take them back again? Let's be cool and consult with Mac and Jablesh."

# CHAPTER 44 – CRUNCH

The next morning, after discussing the situation with Preacher and Red, Mac stood outside the doorway to Jablesh's hidden home, waiting to be invited inside. Jablesh came out to meet him, but for the first time, did not invite Mac inside.

"Good morning, Mac. Is there something we need to discuss?

"We completed the transfer of our endangered species program animals to zoos, but we have a complication. Crunch refused to come back to Hallywalooly. He stayed at the primary zoo to work with animals as a zookeeper. We now have a Dropper living among surface world people."

"That is unexpected and unusual."

"What would you have us do about this situation?"

"That is for you to decide, Mac."

"Jablesh, are you implying that you will accept whatever decision I make?"

"Every decision has consequences, including some we cannot foresee." Without further comment, Jablesh turned and went back into his home.

Mac left, knowing he was stuck with the childhood game's hot potato. He could discuss Crunch's desertion with Merrilong, but the final decision would be his. What would be the consequences of having surface people living with someone who had been revived after death, but who was not truly alive? Crunch had worked with the sanctuary animals, and they accepted him. Could he thrive among living people without causing some kind of problem?

Mac invited Red, Preacher, and Merrilong to join him in the home meeting room for a discussion before he announced his decision.

Once all four of them were seated at the triangular table, Mac said, "Jablesh has given me the responsibility for dealing with Crunch. First, I would like some input from you. Merrilong, do we have a precedent? Have other Droppers abandoned Hallywalooly for a surface existence?"

"I know of only one case somewhat similar to this. Many years ago, a Dropper who had lived in an earlier time period left us to dwell in a modern city, but he did not last long on the surface. The pace of life in the city was too chaotic for him, so he jumped from a high window and died within one month of his departure. Oddly, he had also committed suicide the first time he died; playing a game he called Russian Roulette."

Preacher expressed confusion. "In my old topside gang days I would have answered abandonment with violence. I'm different now, so I'm not sure. The surface world folks might treat Crunch as a zombie if they discover he's not like them."

Mac asked, "Red, do you have an opinion or comment?"

"Only that I was the unique person as a Stopper helping out with post-hurricane rebuilding and truck driving in the Topper world. In both situations, I was accepted as one of them. Perhaps Crunch will be too. However, I am bothered because his leaving violates our past rules. Mac, I feel more comfortable when we follow tradition. It's even strange to me that you're chairing this meeting instead of Jablesh."

"Apparently, Jablesh wants to delegate responsibility for some matters so that he can concentrate on others. My decision regarding Crunch is that he will be allowed to remain on the surface until he wishes to return. We may learn something about letting other Droppers go topside in the future."

Preacher disagreed. "When word of this decision gets out, you may have many Droppers wanting to move to the surface world. People who have died and been revived don't belong there. Droppers, if identified, would be seen as zombies and attacked."

Merrilong stood and looked at Mac. "Something has happened. I sense Hollywing from the Intelligence Center waiting outside to come in."

"Greet her and bring her into our meeting."

When Hollywing entered, she said, "Excuse me for interrupting your meeting, but we may have a major problem. Merrilong told me that you are discussing the decision by Crunch to remain on the surface and work at the zoo where you delivered our animals. That situation has changed. We intercepted a news bulletin that one of the zookeepers there was attacked by a lion and is in critical condition."

Mac frowned. "Do you think that person is Crunch?"

"Has to be. The story said that the victim's blood was green."

"Are you telling me that all Droppers have green

blood? Merrilong, you never told me that."

"I thought you knew. You treated Preacher and Crunch for gunshot wounds during that Jacksonville gang standoff."

"That took place in the dark. I didn't see their blood."

Preacher said, "I look weird when I cut myself shaving. I hope Crunch recovers, but this may be the answer to my question about Droppers abandoning Hallywalooly for the surface. Droppers there would be in constant fear of getting injured and bleeding green blood."

Hollywing said, "Excuse me for a minute. One of my assistants is outside wanting to talk with me."

When Hollywing returned, she was smiling. "We are out of trouble for the time being. We learned that a specialist at the hospital where they took Crunch believes he has a rare disease called sulfhemoglobinemia. That disease makes blood green by causing irreversible binding of sulfur to hemoglobin in the red blood cells. It's a rare, but explainable, reason for a human Topper to have green blood."

Mac addressed Preacher's earlier comments. "This rare disease will free Crunch from appearing weird if he recovers. It also says that we can't have many Droppers on the surface world, or the disease will suddenly become common."

Merrilong said, "Mac, you are a Topper and a healer's assistant. You could visit Crunch in the hospital and heal him."

"That would cause more problems. In Hallywalooly, we heal people immediately. The doctors and reporters would have many questions if a man attacked by a lion healed that quickly. Crunch will have to rely on normal human medical skills if he is to regain his health."

# CHAPTER 45 – DOUBLE DATE

Mac set down his empty coffee mug, pleased with himself for having requisitioned it for familiarity and comfort. There were a few topside touches that increased the livability of Hallywalooly. As Merrilong entered the kitchen, he asked, "Are there places people go in Hallywalooly to just relax and socialize?"

"Sometimes people walk in the garden area."

"I thought of that one. Are there any others?"

"For physical improvement, people hike the tunnels and caverns and climb rock formations."

"On the surface, we have restaurants, night clubs, movie theaters, and sporting events for leisure time outings."

"We have never needed those things here. Are you bored?"

"No, but I promised Preacher that we would spend an evening with him and Trisha."

"We could invite them here, or we could go to their home."

"On the surface, when two couples go out somewhere for a relaxed evening, it's called a double date. I would like the four of us to have one of those."

"We do not actually have a suitable place to go for

that."

"Well, Merrilong, times are changing in Hally-walooly. Send a message to Preacher and Trisha that we will be taking them out for dinner and will pick them up at artificial sunset time."

"Mac Blackwell, you have spent too much time with Jablesh. You are practicing hiding your thoughts, the way he does."

"I want this to be a pleasant surprise for all of you, so indulge me a small amount of privacy."

Just as the artificial sunlight started to dim, Mac's utilizer vehicle pulled up to the doorway of Preacher and Trisha's home. Mac jumped off the motorized cart and rang the doorbell that had surprised him earlier. He enjoyed listening to the doorbell's ring echoing off the rock chamber walls inside. Trisha was the first to come out, followed by Preacher in his cowboy hat.

Trisha noticed Mac's glance at the hat. "My cowboy needs to learn how to clean that hat. It's getting ripe after all the time he spent with the zoo animals."

"I'm wearing it in solidarity with Crunch. Hollywing has monitored his progress at the hospital. He's still hanging in there, but no major recovery yet."

Merrilong said, "You both look fine. Mac claims he is taking us out to a restaurant, but there is no such place in Hallywalooly."

Preacher looked at Mac's grin. "I have the feeling that there will be a restaurant after this evening. Mac is reshaping this place."

They climbed onto the utilizer and Mac moved it forward smoothly. When the vehicle next came to a stop, it was on the broad square in front of the Requisition Center.

Mac said, "You ladies stay here for a few minutes. Preacher, come on in with me."

Less than ten minutes later, Preacher and Mac emerged from the facility carrying tables and chairs. After a few additional trips, three round tables, each seating four people were arranged neatly in front of the Requisition Center.

Mac said, "Welcome to Hallywalooly's first restaurant, Chez Mac. Now, everyone go inside and order your dinners at a requisition station. The best thing about this restaurant is that you may have any food you want. Merrilong, do you want local food or surface world food?"

"Order something for me that they eat on the surface. I want to learn about foods you liked before you joined us."

"One sausage, mushroom, and onion pizza coming up. I'll share it with you."

Preacher looked at Trisha and said, "Damn, that sounds good. How do you feel about pizza for us?"

"Fine if it's pepperoni, black olives, and onions."

"How about that plus green peppers?"

"The peppers aren't my favorite, but I'll go along with you on it."

After the Requisition Center system generated the pizzas plus an assortment of beers, the four friends settled down to enjoy their dinners at one of the round tables.

Preacher raised his beer in a toast. "To Mac, for bringing back to us what we enjoyed when we were alive on the surface."

Merrilong said, "This pizza food is very good. We eat for nourishment on an irregular schedule. I am still having trouble understanding that surface people call eating a special occasion and go out to a fancy place called a restaurant for food. I am enjoying eating with friends, though."

Mac raised his beer for a toast. "To friends and relaxation."

Trisha agreed. "I'll give that a big Amen. I couldn't ever see myself liking a gang member, but I have to admit that Preacher truly has changed. When you're a Dropper, death improves you."

Preacher laughed. "How has it improved you, Trisha?"

"I'm so improved that I now like green peppers on my pizza. The Requisition Center turns out great food. We'll have to eat here frequently."

Mac said, "I have a feeling that when we next come, we'll see others eating here too. News of something unusual spreads rapidly in Hallywalooly. Right, Merrilong?"

"Yes, and I will be coming back so you can teach me about other favorite foods. I never heard of pizza, but now I will want more of it."

Trisha raised her beer. "A toast to favorite foods and Chez Mac, where we can eat any food we want."

# CHAPTER 46 – SUMMERLY

Mac mentally congratulated himself the next morning as he drank his coffee. *Inventing the first restaurant in Hallywalooly was a great advance for this place. Everyone needs to take a break sometime.*

Merrilong walked into the kitchen and gave him a top quality kiss.

"Thank you, but what did I do to deserve such loving treatment?"

"You introduced me to pizza. That was so different from anything I have eaten before. I can still taste it in my mind."

"By using the Requisition Center I'll be able to let you eat many foods you never had before, but I'm sure pizza will be a frequently repeated favorite."

Merrilong held up her hand in a pause gesture. She appeared to be concentrating intently. When she finally relaxed, she said, "Finish your coffee, Mac. Summerly wants to see you in her healing studio."

"You read her thoughts over such a long distance?"

"I am more sensitive than most, but Summerly has special powers, including the ability to project her thoughts over a long distance. She apparently needs to work with you on something important. It would not be wise to keep her waiting long."

Mac took a final swallow of coffee. "I'm on my way."

When Mac reached Summerly's studio, he parked his utilizer and entered, expecting to find her alone. He was only slightly surprised when he heard her talking with Jablesh. Mac positioned himself so that Summerly could see him and waited for an invitation to join their discussion.

The invitation came from Jablesh who was facing away from Mac. "Do not wait out there. Come in and join us."

"I'll never get used to thought-reading, even though I'm beginning to do a bit of it myself. Summerly summoned me for something important."

"I did, Mac. That is what Jablesh and I have been discussing. I will let him summarize the matter."

Jablesh nodded once in thanks to Summerly for her courtesy. "The problem is Crunch being in the surface hospital with his green blood. You will have to go there and do something about it."

"I thought of that earlier, but if I were to go there and immediately heal him from all the lion attack injuries, that would cause more attention than the green blood. I didn't even know that Droppers had green blood before Crunch's injuries."

Jablesh said, "Now you know that, so it is time to take action."

"What can I do? One of the doctors has explained the different color as being due to a rare disease, sulfhemoglobinemia."

"That was a preliminary diagnosis. We have learned that they plan tests to confirm their theory. We need to avoid those tests."

"Fine, but what can I do to stop them?"

Summerly rejoined the conversation. "I will give you an additional two healing powers. You will be my only assistant to have them. The first will be the power to turn Crunch's blood from green to Red. This transition will take place over several hours, so that it will appear to be a natural process."

"Will this be a change in color only, or will the result be normal blood?"

"It will be normal blood."

"Does that mean that Crunch will be fully alive again?"

Jablesh smiled at Summerly. "I told you he is astute."

Summerly did not return Jablesh's smile. "That brings us to your second new power, Mac. Once you have initiated the blood color change, you will perform a reverse healing that will cause Crunch to succumb to his injuries. He will get weaker and soon will die once more, this time permanently."

"You're asking me to kill my friend. Why can't we give him normal blood and then leave it up to the hospital doctors to try to heal his wounds?"

Jablesh spoke in a serious but sympathetic tone. "You proved your friendship by allowing Crunch to remain in the surface world. If the lion had not attacked him, he would have continued to enjoy his new situation. We are simply asking you to do what is necessary to protect Hallywalooly. We cannot take a chance on his revealing our society, accidentally or not."

"I understand. I don't like it, but I understand."

"As I said earlier, every decision has consequences, including some we cannot foresee. Now, I'll leave you with Summerly for your additional healer training."

After Jablesh left, Summerly led Mac into the inner room of her studio and motioned for him to sit down. She said, "As before, extend your hands, palms up, and I will blow on them to open your pores for receptiveness."

Her breath was warm and gentle on his hands.

Continuing, she said, "Now, open your mouth, so that I may fill it with my breath."

From a distance of six inches, she blew gently into his open mouth. He felt tingling on his tongue and gums.

Summerly extended her hands, palms up. "Now, blow on my hands with our mingled breaths as I have blown on yours."

Mac gently blew on her palms and fingers.

Summerly smiled her approval. "Finally, hold your opened-pore palms against my opened-pore palms; close your eyes; and listen for the benediction of the Ancient Ones."

As their palms leaned against each other, Mac heard words in a strange language, even though Summerly's lips did not move. The distant voice changed from female to male tonal quality, and as it did, he began to understand the words. *Heal through wisdom; heal through loving; direct healing with your mind. Know when healing is permitted; know when unhealing is kind. Be a trainer; be a teacher; for your skills to be refined.*

The unmouthed voice ceased speaking. Mac felt Summerly remove her palms from his. When he opened his eyes, she appeared to be slightly older in complexion and hair color.

She noticed his stare. "My change in appearance is temporary, signifying that I have passed a portion of my skills to you. I will recharge to my former energy and appearance levels. Welcome, Mac Blackwell; you are now a junior healer, with new skills and the ability to refresh your healing powers with the hand spray after blowing on your own palms." Summerly handed him a container of the precious spray. "You will not be able to prepare your own spray solution until you become a certified healer. I have no doubt you will reach that level. I find you highly qualified."

"Thank you. I did not realize adding my needed skills would elevate me to junior healer status. You said I would be your only assistant with these powers."

"By themselves these additions did not elevate you. Your understanding of the benediction from the Ancient Ones qualified you. Now, go visit Crunch, and do what is necessary there. Your mind will now be able to control the pace of each healing or unhealing process."

Before leaving Hallywalooly, Mac called on Preacher and told him that his visit to Crunch at the hospital was imminent. "I need one thing from you before I go."

"What's that?"

"I don't know Crunch's last name. I'll need that in order to ask for directions to his room."

"Preacher said, "In gang days, we only used first names or nicknames to minimize impact of our deeds on our families. It became a habit. Crunch's family name is Edwards, and mine is Clark, because I was found abandoned as a baby on Clark Street in Chicago. I don't even know Crunch's real first name. He's always been Crunch."

"I'm curious. What's your real first name?"

"You'll never get that one out of me. I hate my birth name. I'll always be Preacher."

Mac thanked him and left to visit Crunch. *Preacher doesn't know I can read thoughts. I'd probably use a nickname too if Ignatius was my name.*

Once topside, Mac rented a Jeep to drive to the hospital. It felt good to drive again. Upon arrival, he asked for Crunch Edwards' room and was given a stiff-lipped smile by the receptionist.

"Mr. Edwards was in the Intensive Care Unit until late yesterday afternoon. You will be his first visitor in his new room." She gave Mac directions to Room 239.

He opened the door slowly, not knowing whether Crunch would be asleep. A slight wave of an arm with fingertips protruding from a cast told him that Crunch was awake.

"Hi, Mac; I feel like a mummy with all the bandages and casts they have on me. I guess I didn't show that lion enough respect. She did a job on me."

"Maybe she thought she had to protect her cubs from someone as big as you."

"Now that you mention it, she did have a cub with her. You could be right. Anyway, I'm back in a normal room, and it's boring without medical people hovering over me all the time. Thanks for coming."

"I'm going to do a couple of healing things for you to make you more comfortable. You'll continue to be treated by the doctors here, but you'll be calmer and more relaxed."

"They were really bothered by the color of my blood, but I didn't tell them anything about why it's green."

"Crunch, they'd be more bothered if you told them you already died once. But then, they probably wouldn't believe you. I'm going to poke your finger with a pin to get a drop of blood out. Then I'll make it gradually change color from green to red, so they won't continue to be upset about it."

Mac withdrew a safety pin from his pocket, opened it, and stabbed Crunch's index finger. A large drop of green blood formed. Mac pressed his index finger into the blood drop and concentrated on its change in color and normality, while in the background of his thinking adding a time period of twenty-four hours. He would be long gone from the hospital when they observed the color change. When Mac removed his finger from Crunch's he saw a slight shift in the blood smudge color toward gray.

Crunch straightened his posture on the bed. "I'm already feeling more like my old self again."

Mac nodded, knowing that his next step would be difficult to carry out calmly. "Now, I'll give you a minor healing to make your broken bones mend better. Beyond that, you'll have to depend on surface world medicine."

"I know what you mean, Mac, but I'm feeling more and more part of the surface world again. I won't be coming back to Hallywalooly, but I won't tell anyone about it either."

*No, you won't, Crunch; we'll miss you.* Mac placed both hands on Crunch's head and concentrated on an unhealing process, allowing four days for its full development and including an immediate severe case of laryngitis. Then, he waved to Crunch and left the room. Crunch coughed several times as Mac left.

When Mac reached the reception desk, he smiled at the woman sitting there and projected the memory loss effect that Merrilong had taught him. Then, he removed the page with his signature from the sign-in clipboard and departed. He didn't want anyone at the hospital to connect him with changes in Crunch's condition.

# CHAPTER 47
# – JABLESH

The next morning, Merrilong noticed Mac taking a long time drinking the coffee he usually enjoyed and drank rather quickly. When he refilled his coffee mug and returned to pensively staring at a wall, she decided he needed a discussion with her.

"Mac Blackwell, you are not your normal self this morning. Were you able to use my memory erasure thought technique on your trip to see Crunch?"

He reacted by turning to her with a smile. "I can't get mired in my own thoughts when you call me by my full name. That means I've earned a bit of your disapproval. If we were in the surface world and married, you would be Merrilong or Merri Blackwell. Would you like me to use that full name at times?"

"I would love it. Merri Blackwell confirms that I am yours and you are mine. Do it whenever you wish. Repeating my question, did you use memory erasure, and did it assist your mission?"

"I did use it, and it worked quite well. No one at the hospital will remember that I was there."

"Will Crunch go back to being a zookeeper soon?"

"I'm afraid not. Crunch's rejuvenated time as a Dropper is about to end."

"This was your decision?"

"No. Jablesh made the decision. I carried it out, with the aid of new powers from Summerly."

"That must have been difficult for you. Crunch is your friend."

"That's part of my moodiness this morning. The other part is that I feel myself changing as I'm given additional responsibilities and powers. You may not want me for your mate before long."

She hugged him and held him close. "Do not doubt my love, Mac. As you know, I have been here for a very long time, and I have never before pledged to be a mate forever. When I said forever, I meant it."

He kissed her several times. "That is important, Merri. I'll need your love, help, and support. I didn't tell you, but I've become a junior healer, not just an assistant."

She pulled back out of the hug and held his shoulders with her extended arms. "No Topper has become a junior healer before."

"During the process of becoming a healer, I also discovered that I can understand the language of the Ancient Ones."

"Only Jablesh and Summerly know that language. I have never been able to comprehend it."

"I didn't study it. The unintelligible words simply became clear to me. I'm not sure whether my new knowledge will be a blessing or a curse, but I will soon find out."

"How?"

"I plan to visit Jablesh to report on the results of my mission. We know that he conceals his most private thoughts by thinking in the language of the Ancient

Ones."

"He will not be able to hide his thoughts from you. Be sure to act as though nothing is different from before."

"It might be easier to mask my thoughts if I was concentrating on the sex I just had with my mate."

Merrilong took his hand and led him to the bed.

While Mac waited outside Jablesh's home for admission, he felt much more relaxed than he did earlier. *I'm the only one she ever took as a forever mate.* Somehow, that success was far more important than becoming a healer.

Jablesh came to the entrance and invited him inside.

Mac sat at the small triangular table and waited while Jablesh brought him some day-old coffee. When it arrived, he discovered that it was as good as the fresh coffee he had consumed earlier. Jablesh appeared to be waiting for him to speak first.

"I came to report that I have carried out your wishes. Crunch's blood by now is changing color from green to red. He is weak and will be fading. He will die soon. I gave him a bad case of laryngitis so that he could not speak about Hallywalooly, even if he wanted to."

"That laryngitis was a good idea." *He is developing the leadership skills he will need.*

Mac did not reveal that he understood Jablesh's thought. "Because of my friendship with Crunch, I would appreciate it if you and Summerly concealed my part in carrying out your wishes. If anyone here asks about my visit, I'll say that Crunch was doing well when I left him, and will treat news of his later death as a surprise. I'll ask Merrilong to do the same."

"You do realize that lies by omission of information are still lies." *But they are sometimes required of a leader.*

"Of course, but I am concerned about my standing in the eyes of other friends."

*Leadership and friendships are frequently incompatible.*

Jablesh expressed his sympathy and understanding regarding Mac's outlook. He also indicated that he would advise Summerly to treat what Mac did during his hospital visit as confidential. Then he stood, indicating that the meeting was over, and Mac returned home.

# CHAPTER 48
# – CRUNCH

Shortly after returning from his surface hospital visit, Mac told Preacher and Trisha that he had done what he could for Crunch and that their friend would have to rely on the doctors in the hospital for further treatments.

Eight days passed before Hollywing, Chief Guardian of the Intelligence Center, notified Mac that Crunch had died in that hospital. Mac was relieved that Crunch had lasted that long before succumbing to the gradual unhealing process. That long interval freed Mac from the appearance of responsibility. The hospital doctors' inability to cure Crunch's massive lion attack injuries would be accepted as the cause of his death.

Mac asked Merrilong about the normal procedure for handling the body of a Dropper whose revival period expired.

She thought about his question for several moments. "We take these events in stride, without any special ceremonies. Because we live in rock caverns, it would be difficult to bury bodies. Normally, we seal the body in a container along with dry vegetation clippings for a month or more. Then we use the decomposed combined material as fertilizer for our farm chambers. It is an enriching supplement to the fish waste fertilizer that we spray from the fish ponds. We recently used this process for the hundred or more people who died when the big sinkhole opened and crushed them under rubble."

"That sounds like something we would never think of doing in the surface world."

"Think again. Hollywing told me that two of your west coast states are starting to do something quite similar."

"If that's the way it should be done, I'll arrange to claim Crunch's body."

Mac drove to the area where Red was doing Guardian maintenance work and called him aside. "I have a new assignment for you. I'm going to rent a van, and we'll go to claim Crunch's body from the hospital. We'll bring him to Hallywalooly through the warehouse and ramp we set up for the animal transfers. Then, you'll be in charge of handling the final composting procedures."

"Guardians usually handle that process. I have done it once before, so it should not be a problem."

"We'll go to get him tomorrow morning. I have preparations to make today."

Mac drove his utilizer to the Intelligence Center. There he asked Hollywing to generate a document signed by Crunch, naming Mac as executor of his estate with the right to claim the body.

Hollywing consulted her computer. "Fortunately, I have a copy of Crunch's signature from the form he filed to join the animal sanctuary program. I remember him calling it Noah's Ark whenever he discussed it."

"Did he sign it as Crunch, or did he use another name?"

"He signed the form as Albert Crunch Edwards."

"Use all three names on the document you're forging, or let's say composing. If I'm supposed to be his executor, I should be ready to refer to him as either Albert or Crunch."

When Mac and Red arrived at the hospital, they were directed to a small door at the rear of the building for access to the hospital morgue. Mac rang the doorbell, indicated his mission to the technician who opened the door, and followed that man inside. Mac was prepared for detailed questions about his paperwork, but he was only asked to sign a *Receipt of Body* form on a clipboard. The technician partially unzipped Crunch's body bag to check the toe tag. Then, assisted by Mac, he transferred it from refrigerated storage to an adjustable height gurney. He wheeled the gurney outside to the van, which Red had open in the rear, adjusted the cart's height to match the van floor height, and pushed the body bag into the vehicle. A final handshake completed the brief procedure.

Red drove the van back to the warehouse that masked the entrance to Hallywalooly, a route that had become routine for him. Upon arrival, Mac remotely opened the warehouse garage door, closed it behind them, and did the same for the internal garage door that hid the ramp descending into the cavern below. Red drove down the ramp as the internal garage door closed behind the van. Once at the bottom of the ramp, Mac transferred to his utilizer vehicle and drove away, while Red and another Guardian unloaded Crunch's body for its final processing.

# CHAPTER 49 – EXPECTATIONS

Merrilong had coffee ready for Mac when he came home. "Relax and drink this. I hope you did not have any problems claiming Crunch's body."

"None at all. They didn't even examine my carefully contrived written authorization. The technician simply treated the body pickup as a routine matter. Do you have a ceremony when the body is fully composted and ready to use as fertilizer?"

"I have never known of one. That is a commonplace procedure for us. I suppose you could have one with Preacher and Trisha if you wish."

"I may discuss it with them. I seem to be going beyond the normal ways things are done in Hallywalooly and implementing my own ideas."

"What does Jablesh think of your ideas, like that restaurant at the Requisition Center?"

"He hasn't said anything about that one. I can read his thoughts in the language of the Ancient Ones now, and they are very surprising."

"What has he been thinking?"

"During my last visit, his thoughts were about my leadership abilities. I remember three of them. First was: *He is developing the leadership skills he will need.*

The second, in connection with lies created by omission of information, was: *But they are sometimes required of a leader.* The third came when I discussed maintaining friendships: *Leadership and friendships are frequently incompatible.* Why is he thinking like a trainer?"

Merrilong hesitated before speaking. "I have seen hints of this in his behavior. Jablesh is working on something he does not wish to share with anyone else. He is training you to take over most of his everyday duties, so that he will have more time for his hidden project."

"But why would he select me, rather than a Stopper like you or Hollywing?"

"My guess is that he wants someone who is familiar with the surface world for some reason."

"We have had quite a few dealings with them lately. If we have many more, it may become difficult to maintain the secrecy of Hallywalooly."

Merrilong gave Mac a lengthy hug.

"Thanks. I always appreciate those. What did I do to deserve it?"

"That was to congratulate you for being chosen as a leader."

"I only read Jablesh's thoughts. He didn't appoint me to anything yet."

"You have been doing his work for a long time. You have also started your own projects like that restaurant, and he did not object. Many others are already looking to you for guidance."

"Am I your leader, Merri?"

"Of course not, Mac; you're my mate."

# CHAPTER 50 – CHILDREN

Mac did visit Trisha and Preacher to see whether they would want some kind of brief ceremony when Crunch's body was fully composted and ready to be used as fertilizer on the food crops. They both decided against it.

Preacher said, "I saw too many bodies during my prior life, but they looked like people. This composting approach may be good for the planet, but I don't want to see my buddy as a wheelbarrow full of enriched soil."

Trisha agreed with him. "I didn't know Crunch very long, and I've been involved with scattering ashes after a cremation, but I can appreciate the environmental significance of turning a body into fertilizer without wanting to see it spread on crops."

Mac said, "I just wanted to give you the chance to speak up about a ceremony. Merrilong says they've never had a memorial service in the past. They take the composting process as normal and part of the life cycle."

Preacher shook hands with Mac. "Thanks for thinking of us. I have to admit that knowing your body will help plants grow sounds better than 'Ashes to ashes; dust to dust.'"

Mac drove to the Requisition Center on the way home and procured Merrilong's favorite pizza to take home, one with sausage, onions, and mushrooms.

As he entered, she asked, "What is that aroma? I could smell it even before you parked your utilizer."

"Aha! I learn more things about you every day. You can smell things at a distance as well as distantly read thoughts."

"While we're eating, I will tell you something else about Stoppers that you really should know if you're going to be a leader in Hallywalooly."

That got Mac's curiosity going, but he didn't try to read Merrilong's thoughts. She deserved the right to explain this new revelation.

Halfway through the pizza, she stopped eating. "That will satisfy me for now. It is time for me to tell you about the children."

"Are you saying you want to have a child soon?"

"I asked you that same question on the day we first had sex. No, I want to talk about Stopper children in general. You see, they are different from those raised in the surface world."

"In what way?"

"How many small children have you seen since you arrived?"

"We were going to visit a school to see children, but we never got there."

"I repeat. How many small children have you seen?"

"I think I saw one at the Requisition Center."

"That is possible. You will not see many more."

"Why?"

"Children of Stoppers are like baby birds on the surface. Bird parents continuously feed their babies so that they grow very rapidly and are ready to fly when they leave their nest. Our children grow much faster than those on the surface, and appear to be much older than their age in years."

"But you have schools for young children."

"Certainly, Mac, but the students in those schools will quickly grow to be the size of surface high schoolers."

"Do they learn faster than surface children?"

"They may, depending on the individual, and our courses are more limited in variety. They are educated for life in this subterranean world, but they get advanced science and astronomy courses so that they will be able to appreciate the Ancient Ones and their body of advanced knowledge."

"Have I seen many Stopper children?"

"Yes. Many of them work as Junior Guardians. It is difficult to tell a healthy child from an adult."

"Merrilong, I'll have to wrap my mind around these differences before we try for a child. It is very different for me."

"That is why I am telling you these things. It would not be fair to plan on children without you understanding how things are different here."

"How many years do Stopper parents live with their children?"

"Sometimes as many as five, but it is varies in different families."

"So Stopper children are ready to live independently in five years?"

"Some are ready earlier. We never have parents living with children who are twenty or twenty-one years old as they do on the surface."

"Wow!"

# CHAPTER 51
# – TRISHA

During their weekly double date at the Chez Mac restaurant outside the Requisition Center, Mac and Trisha chatted while Preacher and Merrilong were inside getting their food.

Mac voiced a question that had been bothering him. "Jablesh selected you for revival as a Dropper because of your skills and training. In life, or, if you prefer, the first time around, you were a weather forecaster on television. There is no weather to worry about underground, so what have you been doing for him?"

Trisha laughed. "To enhance our status we called ourselves meteorologists. Some just called me the weather girl. Either way, I did my best to tell folks whether they needed an umbrella, suntan lotion, or a snow shovel. Here in Hallywalooly, Jablesh has me working on long term forecasts."

"What do you mean by that?"

"Climate change is melting polar ice caps and glaciers more rapidly. It's also causing more frequent hurricanes to hit Florida. Combine these trends, and you have to worry about rising oceans threatening to inundate caverns under Florida."

"So, you're functioning as our early warning sys-

177

tem."

"Yup. I actually feel I'm doing more important work here than I did before I died."

"How did you die, by the way? You were young and healthy."

"I was careless. I was late for a broadcast, and I didn't check all the turning traffic before I dashed across the street to the studio. A hit-and-run driver got me."

"Ouch! That's a tough way to go."

"No worse than getting your skydiving parachute lines tangled. You were lucky to survive that one. I never would have tried that sport."

"And I wouldn't do it again if I were still on the surface. I assume you're tracking trends in your climate change forecasting."

"Yes. I send Jablesh my trend data once a month."

"I'd appreciate it if you'd send me a copy as well. It seems I'm becoming Jablesh's fire extinguisher for any problem that overheats and starts to burn."

"Will do. Preacher said the same thing about you the other night. His version was, "Jablesh is throwing all his problems at Mac, and I don't like it."

"Thank him for being so sympathetic to my situation."

As Mac and Trisha finished their conversation, Preacher and Merrilong returned with lobster dinners for all four of them.

Merrilong stared at her lobster, the first one she had ever seen. "Are you sure there's a way to eat this thing. It's wearing armor."

# CHAPTER 52 – GENERATIONS

Merrilong watched Mac pour his fourth cup of coffee and sit with an unfocused look while drumming his fingers on the table.

She walked behind him and rested her hands on his shoulders. "Something is bothering you this morning. What is it?"

"Don't just rest your hands on my shoulders, squeeze and rub them; it feels good. My problem is that I'm now supposed to be a leader in Hallywalooly, but there are aspects of it that I can't figure out."

"Do not try to work it out by yourself. I am your mate, and I will help you. Tell me what is so difficult."

"Thanks, Merrilong. I'm trying to understand how Jablesh can be a fourth generation Stopper, while Red is a twenty-third generation Stopper, when they both have unlimited lifespans."

"The answer is that Jablesh and I oversimplified our explanations to you when you first arrived. We did not want to confuse you with exceptions to the basic rules."

Mac stood and faced Merrilong with a shocked expression. "You didn't tell me the truth?"

"Please sit and relax. Of course we told you the truth. We just avoided telling you about exceptions from normal under certain circumstances."

Mac sat again. "I'm sorry if I reacted harshly, Merri. Please explain the exceptions."

She rubbed his shoulders while she spoke. "I told you that the Ancient Ones mated with indigenous people on Earth, and that their offspring became Stoppers, having unlimited lifespans but looking like Earth people."

"Right."

"The exception to that rule is that the children of male Stoppers mating with Earth's female Toppers have long, but limited lifespans as do their descendants."

"You're telling me that Red had a succession of Earth mothers in his line, while Jablesh had only three before being born to a Stopper mother."

"That is correct, Mac. Jablesh will outlive Red, although Red will have a longer life than Toppers from the surface world."

"It's still confusing. If Red had been born female, she would have been a female Stopper who could give birth to a child with an unlimited lifespan, even though she had a mother from Earth."

Merrilong laughed. "That never happens. The second exception to the unlimited lifespan offspring rule is that when Stopper males mate with Topper females, their child is always male. Red could not have turned out to be female."

"So, taking things a step further, would I be correct in guessing that while your nightly blood exchanges with me are supposed to extend my lifetime and give me Stopper abilities, the same would not be true for a female Topper exchanging bloodstreams with a male Stopper?"

"That is true. If it were not, a Topper female would, through bloodstream exchange with her mate, gain the childbirth characteristics of a Stopper female."

"I'm beginning to understand. I'll conclude that Stopper males and females who mate with each other do not have overnight bloodstream exchanges."

"Correct. They would have the same abilities and characteristics without any exchanges."

"I'm still confused. Red is a Stopper with a limited lifespan. If he mated with a female Stopper, couldn't bloodstream exchange extend his lifetime?"

"It could. However, we limit the use of bloodstream exchanges in such cases, just as we did not offer a Stopper mate and blood exchange to your Topper friend, Maxine. It's a matter of population control. It was allowed for the first few generations on Earth because we needed more people. Jablesh was the last permitted case of a male with an Earth or Topper mother gaining unlimited life through blood-exchange mating with a female Stopper. Since then, female Stoppers have only been allowed to mate with male Stoppers having female Stopper mothers and to blood-exchange mate with a select few Toppers, you being one of them."

"One remaining question. Have you ever given birth to an unlimited lifespan child in the past?"

"Only once, a long time ago."

"And that child is still alive?"

"Yes."

"Have I met him or her?"

"Yes."

"Merri, who is your child?"

"Flowerling, Red's mate. Remember that we do not cling to our children over many years as they do on the surface. She has been independent since she was five years old and does not treat me differently from anyone else."

"And, as we discussed, she will outlive Red because he has a Topper mother."

"True; but remember, we do not dwell on age or the passage of time as they do on the surface. They are well-matched and happy together. That is all that counts."

"Then, our mating with bloodstream exchange is an infrequent situation and fairly unusual."

"Also true."

"Merri, have you had many bloodstream exchange mates in the past?"

"You are the first, Mac Blackwell, and you will likely be the last. We are a forever couple."

# CHAPTER 53 – RUMBLINGS

Although she thought it had no significance, Merrilong arranged a dinner at the Requisition Center restaurant for her and Mac plus Red and Flowerling. Merrilong knew that Mac wanted to test her lack of special feelings toward her daughter, Flowerling, but she accepted his inquisitiveness as a factor in strengthening their relationship. She also looked forward to tasting another example of surface world food.

Mac requisitioned spaghetti with meatballs for everyone and spent a few minutes instructing the others on rolling the long noodles around a fork. He also mentioned that some people, especially children, enjoyed sucking individual long strands of spaghetti into their mouths. Soon, everyone was enjoying the treat and laughing whenever someone decided to suck a noodle strand into his or her mouth.

While they were talking at the end of the meal, Mac deliberately mentioned the mother-daughter relationship, looking for reactions. "Flowerling, I only recently learned that you are Merrilong's daughter. You do have some resemblance to her."

Flowerling focused on Merrilong's face. "I do not see the resemblance you mentioned. Perhaps I look like my father, but I do not remember him."

Merrilong said, "Your father was an agent from the Intelligence Center. I think he was in charge of scanning surface world books into the computers for retrieval as needed. He was reassigned somewhere else a few years ago."

Mac expected Flowerling to ask questions about her father, but she simply finished her meal and turned to the task of wiping smears of red sauce off her face and Red's. "If you keep eating this spaghetti, your face will match your hair, Red."

"I might try it again. Thanks, Mac, for setting up this restaurant place and inviting us."

"The restaurant is for everyone. Come whenever you want."

As Mac finished speaking, they heard a rumbling sound and felt vibrations in the ground. The dishes on the table were vibrating and jiggling back and forth.

Mac said, "That feels like an earthquake, but they're very rare around here. There aren't any fault lines under Florida. Red, have you had earthquakes here?"

"I cannot remember any, and what we are feeling is different from the vibrations of a sinkhole opening up."

Merrilong started to clear the dishes off the table. "Whatever that rumbling is, I declare our dinner over. Red, you should return to your Guardian group in case repairs are needed. Flowerling, it was good to see you again."

Mac helped Merrilong clear the table as the others left. Then, they left for the Intelligence Center. When they were halfway there, the rumbling suddenly stopped as though turned off by a switch.

At the Intelligence Center, people were animatedly

discussing the rumbling event while others monitored surface world broadcasts and environmental meter readings.

Mac approached Hollywing. "What do your people think that was?"

"We do not know, but it appears to have been confined to Hallywalooly. Broadcasts on the surface have not mentioned anything about it."

"If it was an earthquake, there may be a series of aftershocks. I suggest your people should remain on alert and be prepared to record vibrations in additional events."

"I was thinking the same thing, Mac. Will you discuss it with Jablesh, or should I?"

Mac was getting so used to taking independent action that he had almost forgotten about Jablesh. He decided to play it cool and avoid long discussions. "I think it would be more appropriate for you to meet with him, Hollywing. It would be part of your official responsibility here. I'll learn the results of your discussions later."

As Mac and Merrilong arrived home, she asked, "Why did you deliberately avoid contacting Jablesh about that rumbling we heard and felt?"

Mac winked at her. "I wanted to remind Jablesh that he's in charge here; not me."

She stared at his face. "Is something wrong with your right eye? It closed briefly and then opened again."

"That's called a wink. It's a sign of something confidential between mates."

"I'll have to learn how and when to do it."

# CHAPTER 54
# – JABLESH

Hollywing sent a note to Mac's computer screen indicating that she had discussed the unusual rumbling with Jablesh and that he had dismissed it as due to settling of loose rocks in a distant cavern after a particularly bad thunderstorm on the surface.

That explanation did not ring true for Mac. There had been many other bad thunderstorms and even tornadoes in this part of Florida, and Red said he had felt no similar rumblings. Was Jablesh giving a simple but probably incorrect analysis because he didn't want to spend time on the rumbling phenomenon, or did he have a deeper motive? Whatever Jablesh's reason for the simple explanation, it backfired by making Mac curious about the old leader's deception.

The next morning, Mac camped outside Jablesh's home waiting for permission to enter. After fifteen minutes, Jablesh's brown-robed figure appeared, beckoning Mac to come inside.

Once inside Jablesh gestured Mac toward a seat at the small triangular table. "I sensed your presence as soon as you arrived, but I made a fresh batch of a new type of coffee before admitting you. I decided that it was not appropriate to give you day-old coffee as I did the last time we shared that beverage."

"Thank you, Jablesh. I'm sure this coffee will be excellent. I came because you haven't been seen in public lately. That is quite unusual."

"I have projects that absorb my thoughts and long stretches of time. You are doing the job of responding to daily needs. By becoming a leader, you have liberated me to do other projects."

"Would those projects have anything to do with the rumbling and vibrations we felt recently?" Mac sensed momentary surprise in Jablesh's thoughts.

"I doubt it, Mac. I have been drilling out another room in the wall of this cavern, because my home needs more room, but drilling and tunneling operations are frequent in Hallywalooly and usually go unnoticed."

*Jablesh is using the powers of his mind to suggest that I should not get interested in the source of the rumblings.*

"Do you expect that there will be future rumbling episodes, or perhaps this was a one-time event?"

"Such natural events may repeat themselves once or twice, but I doubt that they would become a normal phenomenon."

"This is excellent coffee. It's better than the kind we make at home."

"My secret is that it is not grown in Hallywalooly or created in the Requisition Center. It is a special blend that I have shipped to me by one of our agents on the surface. I have a container of it for you to take with you. I will make sure that you also receive coffee shipments on a regular basis in the future."

Mac thanked Jablesh and departed for home, realizing that he had just been bribed to overlook additional rumbling events. *So Jablesh causes or at least knows the source of the rumblings. My silence is important enough to him that he's sharing his coffee secret. I'll have to find ways to make him share other secrets. I'm sure he has many.*

# CHAPTER 55 – CELEBRITIES

Mac was enjoying the last sip of his second cup of Jablesh's special coffee when Merrilong entered the room.

"No more relaxing, Mac. Preacher is at the front entrance waiting for you."

Mac put down his mug and went out to greet his friend. "Hi, Preacher. Did we have something planned for today? If so, I forgot about it."

"Nothing planned. I'm hoping you can be my safety valve. Trisha has started to play Bridge with Ben Franklin, Orville Wright, and Eleanor Roosevelt. My mate gets a kick out of hanging around with celebrities. I don't play cards, and I don't do celebrities, so I don't fit in with that group."

"How long has this bridge group been gathering?"

"The three celebrity Droppers haven't had any assignments since we cancelled the Noah's Ark program. They were bored and turned to cards and Trisha several weeks ago."

"Who suggested the game of Bridge as a solution?"

"Eleanor. She also picked Trisha to be her partner. They must play well together because they usually win."

"Have you picked up anything interesting from their conversations?"

"Only that they earlier complained to Jablesh about the boredom, and he hinted he would have something in the future that would more than make up for their being bored now."

"Thanks for that info, Preacher. I'll have to keep my eyes and ears open to figure out the prize assignment he has for them."

"If it's important, I'll ask Trisha to report on gossip that comes up while they're playing cards."

"Thanks, Preacher. That might be useful. How are you at climbing?"

"Climbing what ... a tree?"

"Nope, I'm talking about rock climbing. I'd like to climb some of the rock walls in our caverns."

"They do go up pretty high, and no two are the same. You talking free climbing or using safety gear?"

"We'll get ropes and safety equipment at the Requisition Center."

"Hold it, Mac. You sound as though you've done a bunch of rock climbing before. I've only climbed stairs and one tree. Are you sure I'm not going to kill myself climbing?"

"I haven't climbed before either. Preacher, you're a Dropper. You already died and were revived. You don't have to worry about falling during the climb because I'm a healer. I'll fix you up if it happens."

"I'm worried that we'll both fall and that you'll be too unconscious to heal me."

Two hours later, after obtaining climbing ropes, harnesses, helmets, climbing shoes, carabiner rings, climbing cams, and a belay device, Preacher and Mac stood at the bottom of a cavern that was wider at its roof than it was at its base.

Mac looked upward. "This should be a good beginner's climb for us. The wall slopes backward because of the large cavern width at its roof. We won't be climbing straight up, so we'll have easier foot placement."

Preacher picked up a climbing cam. "I don't even know what this is. I certainly don't know how to use it. How about requisitioning some beer instead and just telling our mates and friends that we climbed the wall?"

"That thing is a climbing cam. You set it into a crack in the rock wall, and then you can step on it to go higher."

"What if there aren't any cracks when we're partway up the wall?"

"Then we have to find decent hand and foot holes, slight ledges and wrinkles in the rock face."

"Thanks, but no thanks, Mac. You're not afraid of heights. You've skydived out of a plane. I may have been a tough guy on the ground when I was alive, but I fell out of that one tree I climbed. If you want to do rock wall climbing, I suggest you get Jablesh to revive a Dropper who was an expert climber before he or she died. That climber probably died by falling off a wall anyway. Count me out for now."

"You do realize that we're doing this for you? You complained that you had nothing to do when Trisha and the three celebrities were playing Bridge."

"Now, I'm complaining that this wall climbing is too risky. Let's go back to the Requisition Center and get a football plus some beer. For today, we can throw the ball back and forth. Next time, I'll get some of my former gang member Droppers for a team. You can get

Red and some other Guardians for the other team."

"Actually, Preacher, that's not a bad idea. We'd have to put a mixture of your buddies and Guardians on both teams to make it fair, and we'd need a long practice period to teach the Guardians how to play football."

"Thanks, Mac. What should we do with all this climbing gear?"

"I'll take it home with me after the football passing and beer session. I may yet need it in the future."

# CHAPTER 56
# – TOPPERS

They were lying in bed together when Mac asked softly, "Merri, are you awake?"

She opened her eyes. "Yes, and I enjoy starting the day with you calling me by your special version of my name. What would you like?"

"I've been thinking about all the people I've met in Hallywalooly, and I think I'm the only Topper I know. Maxine and others are Hallywalooly Topper agents living on the surface, but I haven't met any Toppers living underground with us."

"You have, but you mistook them for Stoppers because they look the same."

"Where did I meet them?"

"About half of Hollywing's Intelligence Center agents are Toppers. Who would be better at advising us about developments in the surface world?"

"That's reasonable. Where else have I met them?"

"Most of our farmers in the agricultural cavern are Toppers. They work with Stopper Guardians there too. In the old days, before Florida had so many people, we raised our crops on the surface. Many of the farming Stoppers and Toppers moved underground with us as the surface population increased."

"And farmer Topper descendants work there too?"

"Of course."

"It's difficult to tell one group from another by appearance."

"We are all people."

"Red and other Stopper Guardians have helped out during natural disasters on the surface without being noticed as different."

"Mac, even when we went to NASA on that mission, I saw that surface people come in many different shapes, sizes, and appearances. There is no one here that would look out of place on the surface. Only the Droppers would have a potential problem because of their green blood."

Mac disconnected their transfusion mechanism and got out of bed. "One of these days, I'll visit some Intelligence Center and farmer Toppers to learn whether living underground for generations has changed their outlooks."

Merrilong disconnected her end of the transfusion tubing, stood, and gave Mac a morning hug. "You will find them just as normal as we are."

# CHAPTER 57 – MORE RUMBLES

When the new rumbling rattled their home chamber, Mac was prepared to act. He took a box from one of the storage compartments, removed its cover, and turned it on. The stylus inside traced a rapidly changing spike pattern on its paper chart.

"Come on, Merrilong; we're going to find out what's happening."

"What is that thing in the box?"

"It's an instrument called a seismograph for recording the strength of earthquakes on a paper chart. I ordered it at the Requisition Center after we felt the first rumbles. I'm going to use it to find the source of the shaking and noise."

They went out to Mac's utilizer vehicle and placed the seismograph on its deck. Mac turned the instrument off, and they drove in the direction that seemed to have a louder rumbling sound. Then Mac stopped the utilizer and turned the seismograph back on.

"When we drive, we get vibrations from the surface beneath us, so I have to stop to take measurements."

Merrilong studied the chart on the device. "We are going in the right direction. The vibration trace is higher than it was before. Keep going the same way."

Mac turned off the instrument and continued moving forward until they reached a point where a tunnel branched off to the right. He stopped the cart and took another reading. "It's higher than before, but I'll go into the side tunnel and take another reading to see if we should go straight or branch off here."

They turned into the side tunnel and advanced about fifty yards to get separation from the previous point. The rumbling sounded louder, but that may have resulted from echoes in the smaller tunnel. They stopped and Merrilong took another reading.

"It is definitely recording higher vibrations here, Mac. Keep going down the tunnel."

They followed the tunnel to its end where it opened into another large cavern. They stopped to take another reading, but before they could, the rumbling stopped. The sudden silence caught them by surprise and left them still yelling to each other when they could have whispered.

"Too bad, Merri, I thought we were going to find the source."

"I expect the rumbling will come again. Next time we should start measuring at this point. I suspect it comes from the same source every time. We have made good progress."

Mac respected Merrilong's opinion, knowing that she had been one of the technical innovators of the Requisition Center. "We can stop shouting now. I like your logic. If we start from here next time, we should end up close to the source of the rumbling before it stops."

Mac reversed the utilizer and headed for home. When they arrived, they found Red waiting for them.

"Hello, Merrilong; hello, Mac. That rumbling lasted

longer than the last time. Do you think there is something the other Guardians and I should do about it?"

"Not yet. We've been trying to locate the source by using this instrument that measures the vibrations and moving it to new locations where the shaking is more intense. We were making good progress when the rumbling stopped."

Merrilong added, "Next time it happens, we will start our measurements from the point where we measured our greatest shaking this morning. That will give us a good chance of finding the source before the next round of rumbling stops."

Red said, "As I told you earlier, Mac, I never felt shaking like this before. I checked with other Guardians who are older than me, and they did not remember anything like this either. Whatever is causing the rumbling may be something serious."

Merrilong agreed. "This is a new occurrence for me too. We should study it thoroughly once we have a better idea of the source location. Some of our cavern walls may be in danger of collapsing. For now, I suggest we go inside for a drink or something to eat. It has been an unusual morning."

As Merrilong carried their drinks to the table, the rumbling began again.

# CHAPTER 58 – TRISHA AND PREACHER

"Damn! My favorite cup fell off the shelf and broke during all that rumbling. Preacher, did Mac tell you what's causing it?"

"He doesn't know, but he's trying to find out. I thought you might have a problem when you got that fancy cup at the Requisition Center. Cups don't bounce well on stone floors, Trisha."

"At least I can go back and get another one."

"Maybe this rumbling and shaking has something to do with climate change. You're the expert on that. Could some part of climate change be causing earthquakes in Florida?"

"I doubt it. The main climate change problem that would affect us is the rapid melting of polar ice caps and glaciers. As the ocean rises, tropical storms and hurricanes are likely to cause more flooding. That's not a great prospect when you're living underground."

"Living is a touchy subject. We're Droppers, and they keep saying we've been revived after death, but that we're not truly alive."

"I don't know about you, Preacher, but I feel like I'm alive. I may have weird green blood, but I breathe, think, and have emotions."

"But, I'll bet your emotions aren't as intense as they were before you died. I feel sober and stodgy. I'm not as dynamic and demanding as I was before that cop shot me."

"Thank God for that. I wouldn't have given you a second look when you were a gang banger. You're almost respectable now. Remember, too that even though we're revived, we're older. Age affects emotions and outlooks."

"I'm not that ancient, Missy. I'm up for a tumble or two on the bed right now. How about you?"

"At least that part of you is still dynamic. And you're getting to be almost gentle in your old age. You're on for the bedroom."

"One good thing about being a Dropper. No more need for protection. They said we can't have kids. We can have sex all day long without worrying."

"Easy, Buster. Don't get carried away. We'll stop before fun turns into something much worse."

"Agreed; but right now it's clothes-shedding time."

# CHAPTER 59 – TRACKING

When the new rumbling started, Red, Mac, and Merrilong abandoned their drinks and rushed outside to remount the seismograph instrument on Mac's utilizer. Merrilong drove to the point at the end of the side tunnel where they had been set up for measuring vibrations when the earlier rumbling had stopped. Once the utilizer vehicle was still, she took a vibration reading and found it higher than readings during the previous rumbling event. She exchanged glances with Red and Mac, who both pointed toward the opposite end of the new cavern. Merrilong drove the utilizer in that direction, stopping just short of the far wall. The rumbling sound was louder than before. The reading at this point was definitely higher than anything they had previously measured.

Merrilong turned to the others and shouted to be heard above the rumbling. "My guess is that the rumbling is coming from somewhere beyond that rock wall, but I do not know where to go from here. There is no opening in the wall."

Red walked over to examine the wall. "I think there was once a tunnel entrance here. It has been blocked by collapsed rocks for so long that the blocked tunnel opening looks almost the same as the cavern wall surrounding it."

The rumbling and vibrating stopped as suddenly as it had started. Following a few after-echoes, the cavern became silent.

Mac had been unusually quiet. He approached the spot where Red was studying the wall. "Red, the fact that the tunnel entrance has been sealed for such a long time suggests that it is supposed to be kept secret. Do you have a few fellow Guardians who can be trusted to work with you to open the tunnel entrance without telling anyone else about this project?"

Red looked around to be sure no one else was in listening range. Then he said, "Since the time when Jablesh told me to be your assistant, I have had no fewer than six Guardians in my group ask me to include them in my work for you when the task is large or complex. I told them I could not openly favor anyone, but that I would remember their interest. I think all six of them can be trusted to keep quiet about a confidential assignment."

Merrilong whispered in Mac's ear, "If there is a question about their keeping the work confidential, I can erase their memories after the work is completed."

Mac smiled and nodded. "Your suggestion sounds good, Red. Bring your special crew over here the next time your workload is slow. Open the entrance to the tunnel, but don't explore the tunnel itself until the three of us come back here together. If possible, after opening the entrance, cover it loosely, so that it doesn't look open from a distance."

# CHAPTER 60 – RELATIONSHIPS

Once they were back home and Red had left, Mac said to Merrilong, "You told me earlier that you assigned yourself to be my mate."

"That is true."

"I've been wondering for a while how you knew that I had agreed to stay in Hallywalooly or that I had been selected by Jablesh for his special assignments."

"I would rather not comment on that."

"If we're forever mates as you said, you should not hide things from me."

"I have to hide this one for the sake of our relationship. I am afraid you will not want me if I answer."

"I've been through wartime wounds, the bankruptcy of my company, a tangled and partially collapsed parachute, plus all the strange-to-me aspects of Hallywalooly. I doubt that your answer will make me turn away from you."

"You may feel that I am not worthy of being your mate."

"Merri, have faith in my love and loyalty."

"I knew about your situation here because I am Jablesh's granddaughter, and I was able to exchange thoughts with Summerly from a distance."

Mac reached out and held her in his arms. "Merri, I've known from early in our relationship that you are older than I am. How much older you are makes no difference to me. You look and act as though you are my age, and I will always treat you as an equal."

He felt her body relax.

"We are still forever mates?"

"Absolutely."

"Prove it by taking this very old person to bed for sex."

Mac soon realized how much his assuring words had revitalized Merrilong. If anything, she now approached sex with him as a glorious honeymoon celebration. They were both worn out and completely satisfied when they finally relaxed on the bed side-by-side.

"Merri, if anything, you're performing as though you're younger than me. I don't think I'd survive if you were truly only thirty years old."

"Are we through with the age discussion?"

"Your age is not important, but your relationship revelation will probably lead to my asking you more questions about Jablesh."

"That is fine, Mac Blackwell. I told you how we are independent and can be objective about our children, parents, and grandparents. Just hold your questions until after we go through our cleaning process. That was quite a workout for both of us."

Once refreshed and in clean clothes, they sat at the breakfast table, he with his perennial coffee, she with an apple from one of the trees in the farm area.

Mac watched her take a bite from the fruit. "This won't mean anything to you, but with the two of us here, I'm reminded of the Bible story of Adam and Eve, with her taking a bite of the fruit from the forbidden tree."

"We had Bible stories in school. On the surface, you studied foreign languages. Here, we studied surface cultures and religions."

"That's right. Jablesh said some agents from Hallywalooly helped write the Bible and other religious texts."

"In case you are wondering, that was before my time."

"So, you're Jablesh's granddaughter, but he was alive for a very long time before you were born."

"That is true."

"Do you feel special for being his granddaughter?"

"Not in the sense of how I relate to others, but I do have a few unusual talents that even Jablesh does not realize."

"Jablesh thinks that you can only read the thoughts of others during crisis situations, but I know that you have that ability at all times."

"True, and you are already showing signs of the same capability due to our overnight bloodstream exchange transfusions."

"What else is unique to you because of your grandfather?"

"You have seen my ability to erase other people's recent memories, and I share a few of Jablesh's ancient memories, but my daughter, Flowerling, does not."

"Give me an example of such a memory."

"Those memories are fragments. While I have no picture in my mind of the appearance of the Ancient Ones, I do remember that they could adapt to breathing different atmospheric gases."

"That makes sense. They wouldn't have had an oxygen-rich atmosphere before they arrived here."

"Remember that Jablesh said there is a colony of descendants of the Ancient Ones on Saturn's moon called Titan. The air there is nitrogen plus methane. They were able to adapt to that."

"That's right, Merri, and they wouldn't look like the Stoppers of Hallywalooly. I wonder what the Ancient Ones looked like."

"I have never seen a picture or drawing of them. They were my ancestors, but I am more closely related to you than to them."

"One final question – have you visited Jablesh in his home?"

"I did not even know where he lived until you tracked him home."

"He wasn't happy with that, but he never confronted me about it."

"Mac, for some reason, he needs to keep a good relationship with you. At this point he has a growing dependence on you, and he considers that very important."

# CHAPTER 61 – EXCAVATIONS

Red and his group of trusted Guardian assistants gathered at the cavern wall previously identified as close to the source of the ominous rumblings. Without indicating the reason for his desired excavation, Red traced a rough outline of the suspected tunnel entrance and instructed his people to set aside the outer rocks and filler material so that they could seal the tunnel again after it was inspected. Beyond the initial few feet of excavation, debris would be removed and transported to the normal dumping area.

The team set to work, identifying the boundaries of the tunnel entrance as they carefully drilled to remove rocks and mineral deposits that had obscured its location. They worked on the initial layers with the patience of paleontologists anxious to find and identify fossil bone fragments. Once the outer layer had been removed and the materials set aside, they used more normal and forceful techniques to open the tunnel entrance. Red had expected the blockage to be no more than four feet deep, but soon discovered it extended to a depth of almost ten feet before they broke through into open tunnel.

While the Guardians were loading rocks and other

debris onto their construction vehicles for disposal, Mac and Merrilong arrived. Mac assessed the amount of rubble being removed. "That amount of blockage suggests that someone expected that tunnel to remain closed forever."

Red agreed. "The blockage extended much farther into the tunnel than I expected. When we deliberately close an unsafe tunnel, we use no more than three feet of blocking material in case we need to reopen it in an emergency. This tunnel was sealed a very long time ago, so the techniques were different. Once our crew finishes removing the debris, we will leave, and you will be free to explore the tunnel plus any branches off of it. I checked all our records, and could not find any indication that this tunnel exists, let alone how many branches it has."

"I'd like you to join us in that exploration, Red. We may find another barrier at the other end or a split into several tunnel branches. It will also be safer in case one of us runs into any kind of trouble."

"I will join you, but in a supporting role. I will check whether side tunnels are significant, and I will be there for safety backup, but you and Merrilong should be the ones who discover anything unusual or confidential. I do not want to get in trouble with Jablesh for going beyond his assignment to assist you."

"Fair enough."

Once the way was clear, the Guardian crew withdrew to wait until they would be needed again. Then Mac led the way into the tunnel, followed by Merrilong. Red followed behind at a distance of about ten feet, in case he needed to rescue the others from a rock fall or roof collapse. At first, they were all able to walk with adequate head and side clearance even thought the floor of the tunnel was bumpy and occasionally cracked, threatening to cause ankle twists and sprains. As they moved farther into the passage, it became narrower and lower, requiring them to move single file and bent over. At one point, they reached a junction. Red decided to explore the branch going to the left, while Mac and Merrilong would continue on the straighter route. As a safety measure, Red pounded a stake into a floor crack at the branching point and hooked trailing ropes onto each of them, with the other end tied to the floor stake. The ropes would indicate where each had gone and serve as an aid to retrieving anyone who fell into a hole in the tunnel floor.

Mac, stooping to fit through the tightening passage, led the way for Merrilong. "I hope this tunnel widens out before we reach the end, or we may not be able to turn around when we go back."

"We will soon find out. I see a very faint glow of light ahead of you."

"You have more sensitive vision than I do. I see only darkness beyond my flashlight's range."

"Score another point for the Stoppers over the Toppers."

Mac laughed, and it echoed off the tunnel walls. "You're actually becoming competitive, Merri, and making jokes too. Our bloodstream exchange must be giving you Topper characteristics."

"I think it is more likely that I am tending to copy the ways of the man I love."

"I'd hug you right now, but there's no room in here. Let's keep moving toward that light you saw."

They continued, walking in small uneven steps

while bent over due to the low tunnel roof. Mac hoped for a larger space ahead because his bent back was aching. At last, he began to see the light that Merrilong had detected. Soon, his prayers were answered. The tunnel widened and heightened so that they could stand normally, but not enough for them to walk side-by-side. At last, they reached the end, where they faced a rock wall with a small window-like opening slightly lower than eye level.

Mac held his face close to the opening and moved his head to see as much of what was beyond the wall as possible. After several minutes, he backed away and let out a low whistle. Then he gestured for Merrilong to view the scene beyond the wall.

She also took an extended look. Then she faced Mac with a strange expression. "Unbelievable, but we have our answer."

"I have three or four answers."

# CHAPTER 62 – INTELLIGENCE CENTER

When Mac and Merrilong returned home, they found a message on their computer screen requesting that Mac visit the Intelligence Center at six o'clock. Knowing that Hollywing would have a good reason for her request and that she also would not be likely to reveal it in advance, Mac cleaned up after his tunnel exploration and made sure his schedule would be clear for six o'clock.

Hollywing was waiting for Mac in the front chamber. "You have someone waiting for you in Secure Room Number One. It is immune to electromagnetic or telepathic monitoring."

"I didn't know there was a way to avoid having your thoughts read by a Stopper with advanced capabilities."

"We do not advertise our advanced technology, so please refrain from mentioning it."

"Understood."

Mac entered the secure meeting room and tried to avoid showing his surprise when he saw the individual sipping tea while waiting for him. "Dr. Franklin, it's good to see you again."

"Just call me Ben and I'll call you Mac. Two friends having a chat. There's coffee for you. Hollywing said you like it better than tea."

"It relaxes me. This is the first time we've met without your associates Orville Wright and Eleanor Roosevelt."

"Deliberately so, I'm afraid. Those two are enjoying their revival in Hallywalooly too much."

"You're not enjoying it?"

"Of course, the opportunity to return from being dead has appeal. However, one must take this opportunity with a grain of salt and ask why Jablesh wanted us here."

"Have you reached any conclusions?"

"I have, Mac, and the results of my analysis will affect you. That is why I requested this meeting."

"I have to admit, I'm flattered that Ben Franklin would be concerned about me. You've always been one of my heroes in history."

"Enough of the history. Let's get to the here and now. Jablesh puts on a good all-wise show, but the fact is that he doesn't understand Earth people, or Toppers if you prefer. He had the strange idea that Eleanor, Orville, and I would teach him to think like a surface person. He still doesn't realize that we're all unique and that there's no answer to his search for universal understanding."

"Why does his lack of understanding affect me, Ben?"

"He wants to be sure he knows how you will respond to an unexpected development."

"That's crazy. He brought you three here before I arrived. You're saying that he was trying to understand my thinking before he met me. And what is his new development?"

"Mac, he had you specifically chosen to come here before you arrived. He had reports on you from others on the surface. As to the new development Jablesh has up his sleeve, I don't know what it is, but he promised the three of us so-called celebrity Droppers that we would have an amazing experience soon."

Mac leaned forward to be sure he heard Ben's words clearly. "Did he say how soon?"

"No; I tried to get him to be specific, but I wasn't successful."

"Ben, I didn't know what to expect from this meeting, but you've been very helpful."

"Then you agree that Jablesh has something planned that will change Hallywalooly?"

"I do, Ben, and I'm not sure how I'll respond to it."

# CHAPTER 63 - MERRILONG

While they were eating, Mac told Merrilong about his discussion with Ben Franklin. He emphasized his pleasure at having had a conversation with Ben and being treated as a first-name friend, but he also summarized the details of their exchange to see how Merrilong would react.

"There was a time when Jablesh was quite open about his thoughts and plans. He was also more popular then."

"Are you saying that the people of Hallywalooly are turning against him?"

"No, Mac, but they are happy that you arrived because you do not hide your actions, and the people who talk with you tell uplifting stories about your efforts on their behalf."

"I don't want to have a conflict with Jablesh. He's been good to me."

"And he doesn't want to fight you because you are his pressure relief valve."

"What do you mean by that, Merri?"

"As long as you are willing to take care of day-to-day problems, he has freedom to pursue any project he wishes, and he does not have to tell anyone about it. You are very important to Jablesh."

"So, you think that if we ever had an argument, I might win it simply by threatening to leave Hallywalooly and return to the surface?"

"Absolutely, but if you did go back, you would have to take me along. You could turn your back on Jablesh, but not on me."

"Interesting thought. How do you think you would fare on the surface?"

"We did very well together on our mission to the NASA Kennedy Space Center. I could even adapt to your ideas of family connections over many years."

"I'll bet you could, but we won't consider my possible return to the surface an actual plan. I'm expecting to stay here for a long time. I've been much more successful in Hallywalooly than I ever was on the surface."

"Mac, changing the subject to more serious matters, what did you think about what we saw from that opening in the old tunnel?"

"It explained a lot about Jablesh's recent behavior and about his desire for secrecy."

"I think so too. I can understand his hiding plans from you, but I have known him for my entire life, and he is no more open with me. It is a disappointment."

"I'll give him a little more time to confide in me. If he doesn't, I'll force the issue."

# CHAPTER 64 – SUMMERLY

Per Mac's suggestion, Merrilong invited Summerly, the healer, to visit their home. At first, Summerly begged off, saying she had to be at her healing studio in case someone needed immediate treatment. She relented after Mac arranged for Red to stay in the healing studio so that he could take any unexpected patients to Mac's home for treatment during the visit.

When Summerly arrived, Merrilong greeted her and brought her into a sitting area. Mac joined them a few minutes later.

As he entered, Mac said, "Merrilong, you should be grateful to Summerly. Her soothing words and touch when I first arrived convinced me to stay in Hallywalooly when I had every intention to leave as soon as possible."

"I thought you stayed because of Jablesh's persuasion."

"He was influential, but Summerly put me in a relaxed mood so that I would be susceptible to his arguments. You've taught me many things, Summerly, but that initial soothing treatment was beyond anything I have learned."

"That will come during your transition from junior

to certified healer. I suspect that upgrading will come soon, depending on your assignments."

"I'll look forward to that. This is the first time we have talked in a home setting. You don't live in back of the healing studio, do you?"

Summerly laughed. "I spend so much time there that I could add a bed and stay, but I do have a home base near the studio. I have to be able to respond quickly in case of an emergency."

Merrilong had a questioning expression. "At one time, did you not live with Jablesh?"

"That was a very long time ago. When he was younger, he had problems adapting his home world organ functions to his human-shaped body. Our living together allowed me to give him treatments whenever he required them. We weren't mates in the sense that you are."

Mac took his final sip of coffee and put his mug on the table. "That long companionship must be why you and Jablesh read each other's thoughts so easily."

"He knows how to lock me out when he wants to. Lately, he has been doing that more than usual. He must have something serious on his mind."

"I've had that same impression. Have you noticed that, Merrilong?"

"I have felt that the few times I have seen him lately, but he has not been around much."

Summerly said, "At one point he told me that he was leaving the public appearances to you, Mac." She stared at Mac as though she was examining him. " I hope that stance does not bother you."

"No, my assignment appears to be handling problems so that he won't have to react to them."

"You have become a major leader in Hallywalooly, Mac, and I know that Jablesh is proud of you."

"Proud, but perhaps too busy to communicate."

Summerly probed Mac with her mind before speaking. "You know more about Jablesh's secrets than I thought possible. A meeting between you and Jablesh is required. I will arrange that for tomorrow. In the meantime, I must return to my healing studio. Thank you for your hospitality today. I enjoyed the change of scene and our discussions."

Mac contacted Red via the computer to come and take Summerly back.

When Red arrived, Summerly added a parting admonition. "Mac and Merrilong, you will soon have to make some very important decisions. Be thorough in your thinking and support each other during the process."

# CHAPTER 65 – MEETING

The next day, as they were finishing their morning meal, Merrilong said, "Jablesh is outside waiting to be invited in. He is earlier than I expected. You bring him in, and after you two are settled in the meeting room, I will go to the Requisition Center so that you will have privacy."

"Are you sure you don't want to join us?"

"He underestimates me, so I will be the dutiful mate and let him continue thinking that way. It is a good tactic."

Mac greeted the old brown-robed Stopper and led him into the meeting room with its triangular table. Jablesh chose to sit in the middle of one of the sides, so Mac did the same on a different side of the table.

As host, Mac started the conversation. "This is the first meeting we have had in quite a while. I believe we need to understand each other's priorities better."

"You are certainly no longer a newcomer to Hally-walooly, Mac. You have become essential to the smooth operation of our society."

"Thank you, Jablesh. I appreciate the opportunities you have given me for leadership and the assignments selected for me up to this point. I currently wonder about the assignments you have chosen for yourself and their schedules."

Jablesh tried to read the young Topper's thoughts, and was distressed to find he could not. "Something is different about you, Mac. Do we have a problem?"

"Only that you have been concealing your activities and that you have lied to Hollywing and to me."

"Perhaps I have not lied, but have only told stories from a different perspective."

"If two is not equal to one, you have lied."

Jablesh was puzzled. *Why are Mac's thoughts impossible to read?* Aloud he said, "And how did I lie to Hollywing?"

"There was no way that you truly believed the rumbling we all felt was due to loose rocks shifting and falling after a surface storm."

"So, the rumbling is a problem for you?"

"It was a puzzle, but it isn't anymore."

Jablesh's expression changed to one of tension and perhaps anger. "How much do you know, and how did you find out?"

"How I learned about some of your activities is not important. Apparently, you're planning to abandon Hallywalooly in a spectacular way. I think you owe me the whole story."

"First, tell me how much you already know."

"Even before you sent Merrilong and me to NASA, I knew that you had a means of communicating with the colony established by the Ancient Ones on Saturn's moon, Titan."

"Go on."

"I now know that you lied when you said that one of the twelve spacecraft carrying the Ancient Ones came to Earth and then left to search for other habitable colony sites. Apparently two spacecraft came here and only one left. The second spacecraft is in a huge cavern that can be reached through a tunnel having an entrance in the rear of your home. It probably holds the communication device that lets you contact the colony on Titan. Your testing of that spacecraft caused the rumbling that shook Hallywalooly."

"Mac, you disappoint me if you explored my home and its passageways when I was not there."

"I would not do that. I found a different way to discover the spacecraft cavern, and I saw an exit on the side adjacent to your home. The fact that the tunnel connected to your home was my speculation, but you just confirmed it by your reaction. Apparently, you have kept that cavern and spacecraft secret for as long as Hallywalooly has existed."

"Very clever. I also told you prior to your trip to NASA Kennedy Center, that I was worried that a future NASA unmanned probe would discover the colony of the Ancient Ones on Titan. You learned of their plans, and I expected to take action to save or hide the colony. You do realize that NASA already has a small helicopter flying on Mars?"

"Yes, and NASA's larger and more sophisticated Dragonfly helicopter will be launched in a few years for its eight or nine year journey to Titan. A helicopter will be better for the colonists than NASA's submarine concept if they are living in caves underground with their entrances under the methane and ethane Kraken Mare Sea. Are you planning to fly to Titan, pick up the colonists, and bring them back here?"

"No, Mac, and that is the hard part. I do not know

how many residents of Hallywalooly I can take with me or how many Titan colonists will agree to leave for some new unknown home. The spacecraft has a limited capacity, especially since humanoid residents of Hallywalooly are larger and less flexible than the residents of Titan would be. They do not have rigid skeletons and can ease themselves into tight places by distorting their bodies like the Ancient Ones. I had to modify the spacecraft over the years to accommodate more Hallywalooly people."

"That's the first hint I've had of the nature of the Ancient Ones. Regardless of their shape and structure, why not simply alert the Titan colonists that NASA is coming and encourage them to hide from the Dragonfly helicopter or to sabotage it?"

"It is time for me to move on, Mac. I am older than anyone else in Hallywalooly, and as my age increases, so also does my difficulty in breathing this Earth atmosphere. The remaining spacecraft gives me the opportunity to leave and serve our colonists elsewhere."

"With all due respect, Jablesh, you are being selfish. Your breathing difficulty puts you at the same level as people living here on Earth's surface who know that they will die sometime in the future. This is a new situation for you, but you have lived longer than anyone ever on Earth, and you should be able to adapt to a new limited-life outlook. You have responsibility for the residents of Hallywalooly, and you want to abdicate that in favor of assisting a colony of beings you don't resemble and who may not want your help. Why should they leave their home because you want to leave yours?"

"Well stated, Mac. I have debated those points with myself. The colonists on Titan do not know of any other place where the Ancient Ones found a suitable location for a colony. They and we are the only survivors of our species, and they retain their original form. At this point in time, the residents of Hallywalooly are more closely related to Earth people than to the Ancient Ones. Some of us feel a compulsion to reunite with those who resemble our ancestors."

"Do the people you plan to take know about your plan?"

"Not yet, but soon. Perhaps sooner than I had planned because of your discoveries."

"Why do you want to take our three celebrity Droppers?"

"You do know more than I thought possible. It would be a great opportunity for them. They would be the first humans to visit Saturn and its moon Titan. It would be a one-way trip for them, but I am sure they will choose to take it. As Droppers, they have only a few revival years left anyway."

"They would have to remain on the spacecraft when you arrive. They can't breathe an ethane-based atmosphere. I'm not even sure that all your Stoppers have retained the ability to breathe alternate gases."

"Thank you, Mac, for reminding me that I will have to test passengers for their adaptability before I go."

"One final question."

"Yes?"

"If you depart in that spacecraft, who's in charge of Hallywalooly?"

"I thought that was obvious. You are."

# CHAPTER 66 – MERRILONG

When Merrilong returned from the Requisition Center, she saw that Mac was still mentally digesting the information he had gained during his meeting with Jablesh. "It appears that you learned more than you expected during your meeting."

"I did, and one of my most amazing discoveries was that Jablesh can no longer read my thoughts when I don't want him to. Did you have something to do with that?"

"I told you he underestimates me. He has not realized that I can hide my thoughts from him, and now through our continued nightly blood exchanges while we sleep, you have acquired my capability to block thought probing. What else did you learn?"

Mac summarized his conversation and Jablesh's plan to take some Stoppers and the celebrity Droppers to Titan before NASA could get to Titan with their Dragonfly helicopter.

"So, Mac, he plans to abandon us."

"He may or may not be successful in encouraging the Titan colonists to explore other planets and moons for a new home, but he definitely won't come back to Hallywalooly. He says his breathing adaptability for

Earth's atmosphere is failing."

"He is not as smart as I thought. He will not be any more successful at adapting to Titan's methane and nitrogen atmosphere. Old age is weakening his thinking. Too bad; he was once brilliant."

"Jablesh also told me that the Titan colonists, like the Ancient Ones, are smaller in stature than Stoppers are, and they have flexible internal structure rather than rigid-bone skeletons."

"I never learned that in school. They played up the Ancient Ones as being wise and almost gods, but they did not go into mundane facts about their appearance and structure. That is quite interesting. Stoppers who go with Jablesh will appear strange to the Titan colonists."

"He also said that he modified the spacecraft to take a limited number of Stoppers plus the celebrity Droppers, so that would affect the number of Titan colonists he could carry on a search for alternate compatible worlds."

"Hallywalooly will be changed forever. Jablesh thinks many Stoppers will want to go with him, but I doubt it. His clearest thought expressed to you, Mac, was that Stoppers are now more closely related to Earth humans than they are to the Ancient Ones. Especially after mating with you, I will have to agree with that."

"That's exactly why he brought me here and why he's leaving me in charge."

# CHAPTER 67 – HOLLYWING

Mac arrived unannounced at the Intelligence Center. He waited for Hollywing to complete a conversation with one of her data analyst Guardians and then entered her office.

"Good morning, Hollywing. If it won't disrupt your schedule, I'd like to have a discussion with you in Secure Room Number One."

Hollywing realized that Mac was setting the highest priority by requesting use of that special room. She whispered a few words to her assistant and then said, "That room is always kept ready for special needs, and I am ready too."

Once they were sealed in the meeting room, Mac said, "Hollywing, you are our most trusted Guardian. Major new developments are coming for Hallywalooly, and I'll need to depend on you for many things."

"You and Jablesh can always depend on me and my Intelligence Center people."

"That's why we need this meeting. Jablesh will be leaving us soon."

Her eyes widened. "Is he dying?"

"No, nothing like that." Mac summarized details about the source of the rumblings and Jablesh's intent to take the hidden spacecraft on a one-way journey to Titan and perhaps farther."

"You have better intelligence than we have here in the Center. I am embarrassed."

"Don't be. Your focus has been on the surface world and how it relates to Hallywalooly. You haven't been spending much effort on internal matters. I'll need you to devote more energy in that direction now."

"We can do that, Mac. What do you need?"

"Until Jablesh chooses to make his planned journey public, you are to keep what I told you today secret. Once his departure is announced, Jablesh will ask a limited number of Stoppers to go with him. I need you to give me a feeling for what percentage of the Stoppers would be willing to go."

"Without my telling my analysts or the Stoppers they question anything about the nature of the journey?"

"That's the tricky part. You might phrase their questions in terms of exploring the oceans of Earth without being able to return to Hallywalooly. If they're not willing to go that far, they certainly wouldn't travel to Saturn's moon Titan."

"That sounds reasonable. I will get right on it."

"One other thing; your results will be given to me only. I want to be the person who tells Jablesh what to expect when he sends out invitations. That way, he won't be surprised if many Stoppers reject his invitations."

"I understand. This also means that our group will report to you after Jablesh leaves – correct?"

"Apparently so. While you're discovering the views of Stoppers, I'll be thinking about my responsibilities in the absence of Jablesh."

# CHAPTER 68 – SUMMERLY

As Mac entered Summerly's healing studio, she called out to him, "Come on in Mac, I have been expecting you."

"You sensed my presence outside?"

"More than that; I know why you are here."

"Jablesh must have told you about his pending voyage to Titan. If so, I assume you're going with him. You're his closest confidant."

"That would mean that you want me to elevate you to be a certified healer so that you will be able to work independently in my absence. That is very logical thinking."

"I have to prepare myself for whatever new responsibilities I will have after his departure."

"Mac, my answers are no and yes."

"What do you mean?"

"No, I will not be going with Jablesh. This is his heroic quest, so he will have to pursue it without major support from anyone else. The tradition on our home planet is that when one expects to die, he or she must do something major in order to become woven into our tapestry of legends. He will take passengers to witness his feat, but he must create his myth by himself. The second part of my answer is yes. It is time for you to become a certified healer, whether I am still here or not. I see challenges facing you that will require those extra skills and resources."

"Will my certification include learning how to formulate the healing spray with the aroma from your home world?"

"Certainly."

"But how much of that can be made? I assume it has an ingredient from your home world in order to attain that aroma."

"That secret ingredient is a drop of blood from a Stopper. It can be Merrilong's blood, or even your own, since you have nightly bloodstream exchanges with her. You will never lack what you need – in the formulation or in facing the future. In any situation, you will have the ability to heal what is bothering you, whether it is physical or mental."

"Thank you for your confidence in me."

"Confidence comes from within. It is only mirrored in the eyes of others. Now I will first blow on your palms, and then you blow the same way on mine ..."

# CHAPTER 69 – PREPARATIONS

Jablesh wondered whether his mental capabilities were failing him. *Why was I not able to read Mac's thoughts during our last meeting?* This thought kept bothering him as he examined the minimal controls of the spacecraft. Most of the piloting would be handled by computers reacting to the thought interface device. Everything was in amazingly good shape considering how long it had sat idle. *Earth's technology has not begun to reach our level from thousands of years ago. The best feature of the spacecraft is the way it fuels itself with hydrogen liberated from water molecules.* His internal thoughts paused as he realized that Mac was waiting for admission outside his home.

Jablesh left the spacecraft and took his private tunnel into his home. Once there, he put drinks on his triangular table and went out to greet Mac.

"Welcome, Mac. No more secrets. Come inside and join me for a cool drink."

"Thanks. I hope I have some information that may be useful to you."

They settled at the small meeting table, and Mac immediately took a drink from his fermented root beer. "It's a toss-up whether I like this stuff or coffee more."

"You concern yourself with liking the taste of foods and drinks. We older Stoppers eat and drink what is required without deriving pleasure from the process."

"I'm pretty sure Merrilong has favorite foods and drinks."

"As I told you earlier, most Stoppers have become closer to human Toppers than to the Ancient Ones."

"I'm forced to agree with you. That is one of the reasons for my visit. I know you plan to invite some Stoppers to journey with you to Titan, so I asked Hollywing to survey the Stopper population to see what percentage would want to go on a long one-way exploration journey, ostensibly to study Earth's oceans."

"What were the results of her survey?"

"Very few were willing to go. Those who reacted positively were all construction-assigned Guardians. Their background experiences made them more willing to face unknown challenges."

"That may not be a bad result. If we manage to convince the Titan colonists to search out a new home, we will need the skills of those construction Guardians for hiding the entrances to the Titan colony and developing the new colony site elsewhere. Did Red or Shorty opt for a discovery voyage?"

"Red did not, but Shorty did."

"That is promising. My passengers will be the three celebrity Droppers plus Shorty and some additional construction Guardians who will work under his guidance on Titan and beyond. I should have room for some of their machinery and equipment too. Thank you, Mac. You simplified one of the major items in my preparation checklist."

"I have one question that I hope you have answered."

"What is it?"

"How is your spacecraft going to pass through the solid roof of that cavern?"

Jablesh smiled. "It is not as impenetrable as it seems. The cavern roof is an artificial set of clamshell doors built when the Ancient Ones were here."

"That was thousands of years ago. You had better get Shorty and his Guardians on board to clear all the sediment and vegetation that will keep those doors from opening. Otherwise, your spacecraft might never get off its launch pad, to use NASA's terminology."

"Good thinking, Mac. Now I will take you on a private tour of my UFO."

# CHAPTER 70 – RED

Once he knew that Jablesh had contacted Shorty about the journey to Titan and about the preparations needed to reliably open the cavern roof doors, Mac sought out Red.

As they greeted each other, Mac said, "Big things happening, Red."

"I expected you to want some help soon. I did not see what was visible from that tunnel we uncovered, but I know it was something important."

Mac told Red about the spacecraft, Jablesh's pending mission to Titan, and about Shorty and some of his people going along as passengers and workers.

"Before that spacecraft can leave, Shorty and his people will have to clear the soil buildup, trees, and plants that have accumulated on top of the clamshell doors that form the cavern's roof. Your job, along with your crew, will be to cover those doors again after the spacecraft leaves and the doors return to their closed position."

"We'll be doing the exact opposite job to Shorty's people."

"Yes, but your effort will be harder than Shorty's."

"Why is that?"

I don't know when Jablesh is leaving, but Shorty has all the time between now and then to do his cleanup job. You will have to bury or camouflage those clamshell doors very quickly because people will see the spacecraft leave, and they'll rush over here to try to find the launch site. If they find it, they'll also discover a portion of Hallywalooly."

"Do not worry, Mac. We will be ready. We will assist with Shorty's uncovering assignment, and during that process, we will set aside many of the original plants and other objects in order to quickly return them to their original locations."

"How do you feel about Shorty leaving? You'll be under pressure to do his work as well as your own."

"We each get our opportunities and our burdens. Shorty has done well and has earned his adventure. Once he has departed, I will recommend someone to take his place. You will be in charge of approving appointments then."

"You will take Shorty's place as Chief Construction Guardian, as well as my assistant. The person you recommend will have your Guardian duties."

"Thanks, Mac. What else can I do for you now?"

"Contact Shorty, and ask him to work with Jablesh to have that spacecraft launch in the shortest possible time so that it won't be detected easily. They might even determine whether it can launch during stormy surface weather, so that fewer people will notice it."

"Good idea, even though it will make our cover-up of the clamshell doors more difficult."

# CHAPTER 71
# – NASA

Jerry Arkinthorpe enjoyed the view across Kennedy Space Center as he sat drinking coffee with his supervisor, Dr. Hargraves.

"I've been a little on edge about something, Doc."

"What's your problem?"

"We've opened the floodgates to a whole bunch of private companies designing and testing space rockets and then trying to sell them to NASA. Some of them are great, and some are nothing but dangerous. They're not nearly as careful as we are with safety concerns."

"Private industry developers save the government huge amounts of money, and they move forward more quickly than we ever did."

"That's because they're building on the designs and experience data we furnish them. If we had even a few of their explosions and crashes, Congress would insist we investigate the causes for at least a couple of years without launching missions in the meantime. These private firms have an explosion and try again in a month after only a cursory examination of the causes."

"You just argued against yourself, Jerry. One of the best reasons for using private developers is that they absorb the cost of problems and take the blame for their failures too. We can minimize the financial support we give them until they prove they have a working system."

"But we lose control. They can use a privately developed spacecraft for profit-making applications of their choice. We can't stop them."

"There's still flight approval required through FAA/ AST, otherwise known as the Office of Commercial Space Transportation."

"They give serious oversight now, but as more and more companies get involved and flights become more frequent, that agency will become a rubber stamp approver, because they won't have enough funds or people to continue doing a diligent job."

"By the time we get to that point, safety issues will have been minimized." Dr, Hargraves stood. "Sorry, Jerry, I have to leave now. Good discussion, but I have a meeting with two Congress members on the committee that sets our budget."

# CHAPTER 72 – DEPARTURE

Jablesh had not announced a definite day or time for his departure because he wanted life in Hallywalooly to continue in as normal a way as possible. Another reason for his withholding launch specifics was his agreement with Mac to depart during a storm in order to minimize the probability of observation by surface individuals and agencies. Launch of the huge triangular spacecraft awaited Trisha's forecast of a suitable concealing weather event.

At last, she sent word to Jablesh, via Mac, that the next evening's weather should feature tropical rainstorms that normally would have cleared during the hot daylight hours. These showers would be coupled with minimal light from a waning crescent phase of the moon.

Shorty and Red confirmed that the surface clearing of the clamshell roof doors had been completed and that plans for rapidly re-covering them after launch were in place.

The three celebrity Droppers plus Shorty and his Guardian Crew joined Jablesh on board, stationing themselves in seats designed and installed by Jablesh for bone-skeleton humanoids.

Mac monitored the launch from the Intelligence Center, Hollywing having installed cameras in the spacecraft cavern after she learned of the pending flight.

Red remotely triggered the opening of the roof doors from a safe position in the tunnel they had opened earlier to discover the spacecraft cavern.

Jablesh signaled that everything was ready and used the thought interface device to trigger the launch.

The Spacecraft generated surprisingly little noise as it sprang upward much more rapidly than an Earth rocket due to its unique propulsion system.

The shape and material composition of the vehicle triggered a surprisingly small radar return on the tracking equipment at NASA Kennedy Space Center where Jerry Arkinthorpe was on duty. "Damn! There goes another rocket launched by a private company, probably without government permission. High and fast too. It looks small, but it may be heading for orbit. Whoever they are, they might give SpaceX engineers a run for their money." He texted a request to the Perth, Australia tracking station to locate and lock onto the rocket.

At the control panel, Jablesh concentrated on accelerating to much higher velocity. The thought interface device responded immediately.

Jerry Arkinthorpe's telephone rang. "Jerry, this is Dan O'Hearne at Perth Tracking. We couldn't lock onto your object. We tracked it to a point where it disappeared. It either disintegrated or it did the Star Trek thing and went to warp speed. What was it – a UFO?"

"Damn! I never considered that possibility."

# CHAPTER 73 – NEW NORMAL

With Jablesh gone, Mac expected a major increase in the number of Hallywalooly residents that would be approaching him for guidance and solutions to their problems. He was pleasantly surprised when it didn't happen. He expressed his feelings to Merrilong.

She looked amused. "Mac, Jablesh never was an active leader. We have been here a very long time, and most people developed their own routines and solutions to problems. Everyone is pretty self-sufficient. During recent times, whenever significant difficulties arose, they turned to you for assistance. Very little has changed because of Jablesh's departure."

"I guess you're right. It's a bit disappointing, because I've been trying to train myself to respond to unusual problems in his absence. They may never occur."

"Did you not tell me that there is a surface admonition to never say never. I am sure that at some time you will be faced with a major problem that will require all of our expertise. Do remember that you are not alone. We will solve difficulties as mates, and there are many others in Hallywalooly who will contribute when required."

"Fair enough. Here's a minor challenge. What

should we do with Jablesh's home and the spacecraft launching cavern attached to it?"

"The simple answer is nothing, but you may not be satisfied with that. How about doing nothing in the immediate future, but keeping it in mind in case a suitable need arises for that space?"

"I'll agree with you, Merri. You are a quick and resourceful thinker, and I still have much to learn about all of your capabilities."

"I am glad you realize that. I would not want you to get overconfident when people call you the leader."

"They may give me that title, but I'm still the new kid on the block with much to learn about Hallywalooly and its residents. That reminds me; I told Red that he would be in charge of the construction Guardians now that Shorty is gone. Do I have to post that information somewhere?"

"Tell Hollywing at the Intelligence Center, and she will pass the news through one of her regular sessions on the computer screens."

"This leader thing may be easy after all."

# CHAPTER 74
# – SYSTEMS

During a weekly meeting with Red, Mac indicated that he wanted to know more about the systems that made Hallywalooly work for so many years without constant maintenance.

Red looked a bit baffled. "Our systems work for long periods of time because different groups of Guardians maintain them on a regular schedule. Much of the work is done within service tunnels and hidden chambers, so that most people do not notice the workers. The Intelligence Center has all of the maintenance records."

"Good. We keep the systems developed by the Ancient Ones and early Stoppers performing well. Do we have Guardians capable of improving the systems we already have and developing new ones?"

"The systems we have serve our needs."

"That doesn't answer my question."

"Our guardians are well-trained and capable."

"Red, you're dodging the issue. Are the guardians charged with or capable of developing new and better systems?"

"No. We guard and maintain. That is why we are called Guardians and not Developers."

"That may be a weakness in the structure of Hallywalooly society. We maintain and prolong old technology, but we don't have anyone charged with applying new technology."

"That is because our systems are better than those on the surface developed by Earth's scientists and engineers."

"You're right about that up to this point, but surface technologies are improving rapidly. We shouldn't get overconfident and fail to discover areas where they are better than us."

"We may need meetings to discuss your new ideas, Mac. Hallywalooly has changed you, but you are changing us too. More people should get involved when you come up with new areas of effort."

"You're absolutely right, Red. I'll give your meeting suggestion some thought.

# CHAPTER 75 – TROUBLE

The computer screen on the wall of Mac and Merrilong's home bore the flashing message: *Mac and Merrilong, URGENT! Meet Hollywing at Requisition Center at Noon.*

Merrilong said, "I have never seen Hollywing flash her messages before. She is very concerned about something."

When they arrived at the Requisition Center, Merrilong and Mac saw Hollywing sitting at one of the outside restaurant tables talking with a Guardian they did not know, while parked utilizer vehicles indicated that other Guardians were inside the Center.

Hollywing gestured to them as they approached. "Thank you for coming so promptly, Mac. Red told me about your large meeting idea, but we have an emergency that will not wait for one. The machinery in the Requisition Center has failed. We depend on it for many of our needs, and it is the reason Hallywalooly functions smoothly without the need for money of any type."

"General meetings don't produce quick responses. Small ones like this will serve us better in urgent circumstances. I don't believe I know this Guardian."

"Glad to meet you, Mac. I am called Sniffer because of my ability to sniff out the source of a computer or mechanical problem. This one has me baffled. I cannot find anything wrong with the computer hardware or software. I also checked the mechanisms and could not make them function."

Merrilong examined the drawings on the table. "Sniffer, a long time ago, I was a member of the team that developed the Requisition Center computers and mechanisms. I will tell you right now that your drawings do not match the current system. These are early prototype drawings. Are they all you have?"

"These are the only ones we could find. The Requisition Center computers and fabrication mechanisms have been reliable for so long, that we thought they would last forever. Somewhere along the way, someone must have been confused or careless and put the wrong set in the service drawings file."

"I will join your people examining the system, but I worked on only one section of the fabrication mechanisms. Others, who are no longer here, handled other subsystems." Merrilong and Sniffer left the others and entered the Requisition Center.

Hollywing kept her voice soft as she spoke. "Mac, this is one of the most serious problems we could have. If the Requisition Center cannot supply our needs, we will have to purchase our supplies in the surface world. Our hidden surface bank balances will not last long, and we will be forced to use counterfeit money that we make here. Counterfeiting is not a long term solution. Sooner or later it would be discovered by the authorities."

He replied softly, "Merrilong will try to get the Requisition Center working again. In the meantime, I'll think about our options if we live without it." Mac hoped his voice sounded optimistic, but he really had no workable ideas.

About thirty minutes after Merrilong and Sniffer entered the Requisition Center to try to repair the system, Red arrived on his utilizer cart. Mac described the situation and repair status to him. Following Mac's briefing, Red said, "I will join them inside. I may have information they lack."

Once inside, Red called for Merrilong and Sniffer to join him. When they arrived, he led them to a narrow service alleyway behind the mechanism assemblies. He slid sideways along that serviceway until he came to an opening in the rear wall that was blocked by a steel door. Red removed a key from his pocket and unlocked the door, swinging it backward into the wall opening. "This side chamber contains spare parts and subassemblies for most of the mechanisms. You should also find backup computer consoles and miscellaneous items, perhaps even instruction documents and assembly drawings. A long time ago, my team excavated the side chamber and filled it with all the stuff you see in front of you. It looks as though it has not been touched, so you should have replacement assemblies for most of the system."

Sniffer patted Red on his back. "Thanks so much. You may be the only one who still remembered what was stored here. Merrilong, I hope these replacements look familiar and you recall how they go together."

"I will need assistance from both of you to remove the old assemblies and install the replacements, but I feel much more optimistic about getting the Requisition Center working again."

After the work was completed and operationally tested, Merrilong returned home with Mac feeling exhausted and filthy. They both went through a thorough cleanup, and then Mac gave Merrilong a full-body massage.

"Your massage process is something special. I never had anything like it before."

"Tight, knotted muscles need to relax after intense usage before they're ready to do more normal things again."

"I'll make sure you have better-than-normal sex in return tonight."

"Now that gives me something to look forward to."

"On a more serious level, that failure at the Requisition Center was close to disaster for Hallywalooly. We are discovering that this is a fragile society. What can we do about it for a long-term solution?"

"I thought about that while you were working on today's repairs. I may have something worthwhile, but quite a bit of preliminary work will be required. I'll start looking into practical details and obstacles tomorrow."

# CHAPTER 76 – SUMMERLY

Summerly sensed Mac at the entrance to her healing studio and invited him in. "Welcome. I did not expect to see much of you after you became a certified healer."

"Quite the contrary, Summerly. With Jablesh gone, I consider you my best link to the ways of the Ancient Ones and Hallywalooly traditions."

"I sense that you are checking on our traditions in order to break a few of them."

"And, of course, you are correct."

"Lay out your thinking. I promise I will not read your thoughts to anticipate your words."

"I will be checking with many people before I take action, because others have backgrounds appropriate to other aspects of normal activities. In particular, I would like your opinion on an unusual healing procedure I would like to take."

Mac detailed his proposal, which was in sharp contrast to Hallywalooly traditions and which would have been a taboo subject in the past.

"And you want to do this because it will help Hallywalooly survive when our systems and technologies fail?"

"That is correct."

"Under those circumstances, I will agree that it is justifiable."

"Thank you."

"You must realize that the bigger question is whether we will put ourselves in this position again in the future."

"I do understand that, and I propose that we eliminate that possibility on a permanent basis."

"Why?"

"Because I will attempt to convince others, in a general meeting, that Hallywalooly should take a new approach in the future. If we move forward in that direction, several hallowed past procedures will no longer be necessary or desirable. No one will again face a death sentence like Crunch."

"I understand. Jablesh needed Droppers, but he never fully trusted them. Make sure I am at the general meeting. I will support this aspect of your efforts and probably others."

"When the time comes for that meeting, I would like you to chair it."

"It will be an honor."

# CHAPTER 77 – HOLLYWING

Once again, Mac scheduled a private meeting with Hollywing in Secure Room Number One. She made sure that he had an ample supply of coffee.

He opened the discussion. "We had a near disaster when the Requisition Center stopped working. I have some proposals that I will present in a general meeting, regarding a new path for Hallywalooly that will avoid future equipment and technology failures."

"Whatever we do, there will be equipment failures. It is the nature of things."

"Let's say that my plans will aim at being prepared for catastrophic failures that we can't repair or replace."

"What can the Intelligence Center do to help?"

"You will actually have the most difficult effort, and it will continue for many years. Here's what I'm thinking …"

"I see what you mean. There will be complications in documentation, among other things."

"I'm sure we will find many additional details requiring extra efforts in the Intelligence Center. Do you think you will be able to handle them?"

"Yes, but I may require additional staff."

"That won't be a problem."

"Then I see no barrier to handling all the details that arise."

"Thank you, Hollywing."

"Some may consider this craziness."

"If it works, it's not crazy."

# CHAPTER 78 – MERRILONG

When Mac returned home, Merrilong looked at him suspiciously. "You are using the thought-blocking technique I taught you. I know you used it to keep Jablesh from reading your thoughts, but I did not think you would ever use it with me."

"Sometimes I feel much more satisfied if you wait to hear what I have to say instead of reading my thoughts before I'm ready to share them with you."

"And this is one of those times?"

"Yes, it is. I need to explain my thoughts for the future of Hallywalooly, and then I would like you to give me your reaction to them."

"If that means you value my opinions, I will refrain from trying to read your thoughts."

"Good. I think we need a totally new outlook, not just to be different, but because it will give us insurance against future technology failures."

"That sounds good so far, although many will argue that traditions are important for preserving our values and our self-confidence."

"In many ways I will agree with them, but we have to identify potential problems and have plans available for solving them."

"Now you are speaking like an engineer."

"That's because I live with one, whether she has a formal document classifying her as an engineer or not."

"Do you like living with an engineer?"

"I thoroughly enjoy living with a fantastic lover who also happens to be a de facto engineer."

"Just so you rate loving above engineering. I may find an engineering problem I cannot solve, but I know we share a great love."

"I couldn't agree more, but we have to get back to discussing my ideas. I need your reactions to them."

"I will be all business during our discussion and save the loving for later."

"Here are some of my ideas at this point.... I know some of them will have to be modified later."

"I like your approach, Mac, but there will be many details that need to be researched for your scheme to work smoothly. My engineer's mind looks at your bundle of ideas as a prototype of something very good, but some wrinkles in the fabric of your thinking will have to be smoothed out."

"I know. That smoothing process will start in the general meeting that I want to convene in the near future. Once everyone knows and gives preliminary agreement to my plans, we'll be able to address specific details."

"Hold it right there, Mac. What will you do if some people object and do not give you that preliminary agreement?"

"Unless someone presents a better set of ideas for us to consider, I expect that at least on a first phase, preliminary basis, people will agree."

"Why?"

"Because the history of Hallywalooly shows that people here tend to go along with their leaders without major arguments. If there is significant conflict, I may be able to handle it as a certified healer. Further, most of my ideas have already been endorsed by Summerly, who will be chairing the meeting."

"Now, I am bothered. You are asking for my opinions when you have the meeting set up for approval, whether I like your thoughts or not. You are cheating."

"If you have better ideas, I will include them, even if I have to drop some of mine. My arrangements for minimizing arguments are simply a matter of speaking from a position of strength instead of weakness. It is good negotiation practice."

"It is cheating. How will you respond to someone with a long history here saying that you are too recent an addition to lead the residents of Hallywalooly?"

"Do you think someone might do that?"

"I might."

"Ouch! There won't be a meeting or proposals for change if the two of us can't agree on their value. I would have to leave if that is the case."

"You cannot leave without your mate."

"Fine. I'll take you with me."

"If you promise we will never be separated, I will not object to your suggestions for change. I agree with most of them anyway."

"Merrilong, sometimes you are hard to understand."

"Thank you, Mac; I will take that as a compliment. I do not want to always be predictable or to feel I must agree with you on everything."

# CHAPTER 79 – GENERAL MEETING

Merrilong greeted everyone as they arrived and directed them to the meeting room with its large triangular table, shaped like the Ancient Ones' spacecraft. The lucky ones found seats at the table. The rest stood, lining the walls of the room, but leaving an aisle so that speakers could stand or walk around while making their presentations or comments. Chairperson Summerly sat at one of the points of the triangular table. Mac and Hollywing sat at the other two points. After the room was full, any overflow people would watch and listen on computer wall screens.

Once Merrilong entered and found the seat Mac had saved for her, Summerly called the meeting to order. "Greetings to everyone. This meeting has been arranged because Hallywalooly is facing potential difficulties in the future, requiring us to consider possible changes in the way we live and operate. The first presenter will be Hollywing, Chief Guardian of the Intelligence Center."

Hollywing walked around the table as she spoke so that everyone would have an equal feeling of personal contact with her. She summarized the near catastrophe due to the failure of the Requisition Center, emphasizing the effect on their society of not being able to get items when required and the consequent need to find cash to buy scarce items from sources on the surface. She finished by reminding people that many items normally obtained through the Requisition Center would not even be available from surface sources because of their uniqueness.

Merrilong was the next speaker. She covered the topic of technology, emphasizing the way Hallywalooly had benefitted from the scientific advances of the Ancient Ones, but noted that new advances in technology had been lacking within underground Hallywalooly while they had been pursued vigorously in the surface world.

A few more speakers addressed personal experiences with requisitioned devices that did not work properly and with maintenance that took longer than expected. Red responded to the maintenance complaints by indicating that the limited resources of the Guardians were allocated on a continuously updated priority basis.

Finally, having exhausted general topics, Summerly called on Mac Blackwell to present his proposals for changes affecting life in Hallywalooly. Many listeners leaned forward to hear better, having received rumors that Mac would suggest drastic changes.

He stood and surveyed the audience. "Welcome, everyone. I am relatively new to Hallywalooly, but Jablesh gave me many assignments to ease his workload and asked me to keep solving problems now that he has left us for the Titan colony."

Hollywing interrupted. "Everyone should realize that for months prior to Jablesh's departure, Hallywalooly was run by Mac, not Jablesh."

Mac nodded his thanks for her comment. "Hallywalooly has been here for an unbelievably long time, functioning smoothly and being invisible to Earth people living on the surface. There have been interactions between our people and the surface people, but they have been brief and have been accomplished in ways that did not reveal our presence. All of this has worked well up to this point."

An older Stopper said, "And it will keep working for a long time into the future."

Mac responded. "You may be right. We can continue all of our past practices as long as we have no further equipment breakdowns or other circumstances requiring us to purchase our supplies from surface sources. However, we know from the laws of physics and personal fallibility that things will fail or go wrong due to careless mistakes at some point. I say we should make a few changes to be ready to handle future problems."

Someone called out, "What kind of changes?"

"There's an old saying on the surface that sometimes the best way to keep something secret is to hide it in plain sight. I suggest that we learn how to mingle with the surface people without calling attention to ourselves by appearing to be different. This will require quite a bit of training and creative documentation, but it will allow us access to the resources of the surface world and will protect our society should climate change ever cause our caverns to flood from rising ocean levels."

Trisha spoke up. "As a trained meteorologist, I can

tell you that cavern flooding is a real possibility at some time in the future. For those who don't know me, I'm a Dropper that Jablesh revived and tasked with monitoring potential dangers from climate change."

Mac smiled at the timing of Trisha's comment. "That brings me to my next proposed change to our society. If we secretly mingle with the surface people, we will want to include our Droppers, but we will need to keep them from being discovered and treated as zombies or worse. Therefore, I propose that all existing droppers be treated by healers to convert their green blood to normal red blood. This will mean that they will change from their revived status to truly being alive for a second time."

All the Droppers present applauded and shouted their enthusiasm.

Mac quieted them. "The second part of my Dropper proposal is that we will not revive any Droppers in the future. There will be no need for them if we can simply work with surface people to obtain new skills, even on the basis of hiring them."

The room was filled with a buzz of people expressing conflicting comments.

Summerly stood and called the group to order. "I have discussed this proposal for Droppers with Mac, and I agree with it. Droppers were a past necessity, but they will not be required under the proposed new changes. Existing droppers with normal red blood will be fully alive; they will have typical human life expectancies; and they will be able to have babies if they are of suitable ages."

Trisha and Preacher could be heard above the crowd noise, cheering loudly.

Summerly again called for order and sat down.

Mac continued. "We are not going to abandon our caverns in favor of living on the surface world, but we will be able to move, unrecognized, between the two habitats. I won't give you a detailed plan for doing that today, but each of you will be contacted to receive your suggested assignment within a major plan that I will soon unveil after further discussions with many of you. Once more, I will emphasize that training to make our people welcome and invisible in the surface world will be required. This training will be supervised by Hollywing and the Intelligence Center staff. They will soon advise each of you as to the content of the training. That is the end of today's meeting, but we will remain available for informal questions afterward."

Summerly announced, "The meeting is now adjourned."

Trisha ran over to Mac and kissed him. "Preacher and I will be able to have children! You're wonderful!"

# CHAPTER 80 – DROPPERS

On the way home, Merrilong said, "Mac, it may not be important to you, but I like things to be logical, so I have a question about one of the changes."

"What is it?"

"What do I call a Dropper who has regained life through the green-to-red blood formulation change? Will those Droppers be the same as Toppers?"

"That's a good question. I suppose we should have an answer for it. We could call them Retoppers."

"That would make it sound as though they were second class or used people."

"They would be having a second lifetime."

"How about Livers or Lifers?"

"Sorry, Merri, those won't work. Livers are organ meats from animals, and lifers are convicts who have been sentenced to life in prison."

"I guess there will not be a good name for them."

"Not so fast – I think I have one. How about Risers? They will be rising from Dropperhood to be fully alive again."

"I like that name. It even has a positive image in my mind. They will be special and will have a name that emphasizes that."

"Risers it will be. I'll start the bloodwork transitions tomorrow if Summerly thinks it isn't too soon."

Summerly agreed and sent out telepathic and computer screen messages to all the Droppers, requesting them to appear at the healing studio the next day for their blood transition procedure. She also agreed to work with Mac on the effort in order to complete it within a reasonable time. Mac accepted her offer, but insisted that he would be assisting her, and not the other way around.

When Mac arrived at the healing studio the next morning, he encountered a long line of Droppers waiting for the bloodstream procedure. Mac had never requested a census of the Droppers, and hadn't realized there were so many of them. He began to wonder whether people on the surface world would be more shocked to realize there were Stopper space aliens among them or large numbers of second-time-around Risers.

Inside the healing studio, Summerly and Mac donned their lab coats and set up procedure stations in two different rooms so that they wouldn't distract each other with their simultaneous ministrations. They had agreed to have the transitions from green to red blood occur over a full day. Summerly's appointed Guardian would allow only one Dropper at a time into each treatment room.

Mac finished drinking his coffee and then signaled the Guardian that he was ready for his first patient. That patient turned out to be one of the former gang members who had been on the street gang mission in Jacksonville. His name tag read Cruiser.

Mac welcomed him and had him place his hand, palm upward, on the tabletop. Then he used a lancet device to puncture his index finger. A large drop of green blood formed. Mac pressed his index finger into the blood drop and concentrated on its change in color and normality, while in the background of his thinking adding a time period of twenty-four hours. As Cruiser left, the Guardian informed him that snacks and drinks were available at the Requisition Center restaurant if he wanted to rest before going somewhere else.

Mac mentally applauded the shortness of the procedure. His only requirement between patients was to change to a fresh needle in the lancet device.

When the last Dropper left, Mac asked the Guardian how many patients there had been in total. He replied that Mac had seen one hundred thirty-seven people, while Summerly had processed two hundred fifteen, for a total of three hundred fifty-two. Mac mentally acknowledged that Summerly was far more efficient. He suddenly perceived Summerly's thought message: *You did quite well for your first time processing large numbers of people.*

# CHAPTER 81 – TRANSITION SCHOOL

At the Intelligence Center, Hollywing addressed those who had been invited to serve as instructors for teaching Stoppers and Droppers how to live unnoticed in the surface world. "As you know, within Hallywalooly, Droppers and Stoppers live and work side-by-side with Toppers who have joined us and adopted our ways. We hardly notice them, because we all look similar and their actions are no different from ours. I am asking you to become members of the new training staff that will teach Stoppers, and to a lesser extent Droppers, how to live on the surface world without attracting attention as being different. Our Droppers lived on the surface previously, so their main need for training is in ways to evade detection as someone who has already died. People recognized as having returned from the dead would cause panic. Avoiding second life identifications will be one of our top priorities."

Trisha raised her hand for attention. "Hollywing, with regard to disguising Droppers, I can help, because I once worked in a beauty salon while I was in school for meteorology. Another Dropper who is here today, Phyllis Jennings, worked as a makeup artist in theater productions. Between the two of us, we should be able to give most of the Droppers appearance makeovers that will greatly reduce their chances of being recognized."

"Great! Note that Trisha also taught us something that surface people do in their schools. They are taught to raise a hand for attention and keep it up until the teacher calls on them. One of the first and most important adjustments Stoppers will have to make before living on the surface is the selection of a suitable name. In Hallywalooly, we have always gone by a single name, but on the surface they use a first name plus a family name, and usually they add a middle name as well, just for confusion. Very few people remember the middle names of others, but it is an optional addition."

Mac interrupted. "Hollywing mentioned that your last name will be your family name. People who live on the surface have deeper relationships with others in their families than is the case in Hallywalooly. Families typically live together from birth until the child is about twenty years old. Usually, all members of the family will have the same last name. Just to complicate things, in most cases, people marry their partners rather than simply mate with them. Marriage is a religious and legal ceremony of commitment to each other. When a couple gets married they usually take the same family name. In a mixed gender marriage, the female usually, but not always, takes the family name of her male partner."

Merrilong asked, "Are there same sex matings?"

Mac said, "Hollywing and her Intelligence Center staff will share detailed materials on same sex marriages and gender variations you may encounter while living on the surface."

Trisha raised her hand again, and Hollywing nodded to her to speak. "I want to know who will perform the wedding ceremony for Preacher and me. Do we have someone legally qualified?"

"The Intelligence Center will issue to each of you a new birth certificate and other documents establishing your identity with your new name. Once you and Preacher have those documents, you will be able to apply for a marriage license and be married by the clergy person or city official of your choice. Our documents are of very high quality and are not likely to be questioned."

Merrilong copied Trisha and raised her hand. Hollywing called on her to speak.

"Will I require two sets of documents, one in my new personal name, Merri Long, and one in my soon-to-be married name, Merri Blackwell?"

"No, you will simply use your chosen married name on your marriage certificate when you get married, and then continue to use it after that point in time."

Mac interrupted. "Hollywing, Merri's question may point out a problem. If the Intelligence Center furnishes a Stopper with a birth certificate and Social Security card, those documents will not be able to be legally updated for a name change and will not be usable when applying for a driver's license or a voter registration card."

Hollywing said, "I did not want to bring up possible complications too soon. We will discuss driver's licenses and voter registration cards later. Let us just say for now that our Intelligence Center has the capability to issue birth certificates and Social Security cards that will match the records of the agencies involved."

Mac laughed. "You're telling us that the Intelligence Center can hack into the computer programs of public agencies."

"That is one of our options. We also have agents on the surface who work for many of those agencies."

"That's even better. Those agents can generate legal documents within their systems."

"You are correct. May we proceed with selection of new names?"

"Certainly; I'm sorry I interrupted."

"Please come to me, one at a time, and tell me the new name you have selected, so that I may record it. I will start. Hollywing will be Holly Winger."

"Merrilong will be Merri Long."

"Summerly will be Summer Lee."

"Trisha will be Patty Chambers. Patty is another nickname for Patricia, which is my birth name."

"Red will be Connor O'Rourke. I read that people of Irish descent frequently have red hair."

"Flowerling will be Flora O'Brien. If Red is to take an Irish name, his mate should take one too, at least until she becomes Flora O'Rourke through the marriage ceremony."

"Preacher Clark will become Paul Cooper. Is Cooper acceptable as your married name, Trisha?"

"It's perfect. Patty Chambers will become Patty Cooper. My initials will stay the same."

"Phyllis Jennings will become Paula Jenkins. I like the idea of keeping my initials too."

The pattern continued as the remaining teacher candidates selected their new names.

# CHAPTER 82
# – LESSONS

At Mac's request, the Guardians converted a large side cavern with a relatively low ceiling height into an auditorium so that teachers could minimize the number of times they presented their lessons.

Mac was the first to take the podium. "Welcome to our training session for Stoppers and Droppers preparing to live on the surface. We will not be abandoning our underground home in Hallywalooly, but you will all soon be capable of living on the surface as well. I will soon announce a major proposal for Hallywalooly, but first I have a few comments that will affect you as you live above ground.

"I believe that you have all given the Intelligence Center the names you wish to use when you live among the surface people. They will soon generate official identification documents for you in those names. However, there will be a slight complication for Stoppers and for Toppers who have undergone the nightly blood exchanges with their Stopper mates. Those individuals have unlimited lifetimes and show very few signs of aging. Because surface people and Toppers without Stopper mates have an average life expectancy of about eighty years, those of you with unlimited lifetimes will have to change your identities and living locations every twelve to fifteen years or so. Otherwise, your neighbors will notice that you aren't aging along with them. Stopper parents with rapid-growth young children will have to claim they are older than their calendar age and will have to home school them because they will look much older than same-age neighbor children. Remember that as people living on the surface, you will be expected to live together with your children for at least eighteen years. Further, those with the ability to read other people's thoughts will have to hide that skill in order to blend in with the rest of the population. Now, I'll let Hollywing introduce you to your teachers for other aspects of your transition to surface living."

"Thank you, Mac. Before I discuss teacher and subject assignments, I want to let you know that right now, our Guardians are building a development of typical surface houses near the warehouse that we have been using for shipments to and from surface locations. After you have completed our training courses, you will have the opportunity to live in one of these houses for a short period before you move to a neighborhood where you will live alongside surface people."

One of the Stoppers sitting in the rear asked, "What if we do not yet feel ready to live on the surface?"

"You will be welcome to stay in Hallywalooly until you do feel ready. We do not want to rush anyone into a lifestyle that bothers them. As to the training classes, they will be taught more than once, so do not worry about schedule conflicts. Attend classes at your most comfortable pace. Early learners will later become teachers for additional training sessions." Hollywing nodded, and computer screens around the auditorium lit to display information. "Here are your training classes and their teachers. We have used the teachers' current names rather than those newly selected to eliminate confusion."

- Family Values and Relationships – Trisha
- Stealth Living for Droppers – Intelligence Center Staff
- Speech Patterns: Use of Contractions for Informality – Mac
- Clothing Styles and Makeovers – Phyllis Jennings and Trisha
- Eating Patterns and Diets – Mac
- Current Events and Culture – Intelligence Center Staff
- Driving – Red
- Sports and Competition – Preacher
- Work and Occupations – Intelligence Center Staff
- Money and Finance – Intelligence Center Staff
- Surface Medical Systems – Summerly
- Surface Technology – Merrilong

Teachers with more than one assigned topic will discuss them in alternately scheduled classes.

# CHAPTER 83 –
# TEST PERIOD

Once classes and construction of the typical houses were completed, couples and small groups were assigned to live on the surface, adjacent to the Hallywalooly warehouse for a two week period. Mac and Hollywing, as administrators of the program, expected to encounter unexpected consequences of Hallywalooly people living in houses rather than underground. The first universal consequence was fascination at the daily sequence of sunrise, sunset, and nighttime sky-watching. When practical, housing assignments for shared residences included at least one Topper or Dropper with surface-living experience to make the transition for Stoppers easier.

Mac and Merri were assigned a two story house with an attic and a basement. Merri was immediately intrigued by the concept of living on different levels. She repeatedly climbed stairs from the basement all the way up to the attic with its pull-down stepladder hidden above a ceiling panel. Once in the attic, she would stand for long periods looking out the dormer window at the sprawling landscape. It was all new and wonderful for her.

She also found the kitchen with its various appliances to be interesting but primitive compared to the food preparation and storage technology in Hallywalooly. However, she vowed to herself that she would become expert at using each device in order to become completely at home in Mac's world.

Most of the furnishings were familiar to Merri, but she found the bed that pulled out of the bottom of a couch to be charming. The windows had curtains on them, but Merri pushed them aside so that she could look beyond the house's walls every time she passed the glass-paned openings.

One day, Mac drove off with Red in one of the trucks and returned with his car, which had been stored in a garage since his decision to remain in Hallywalooly. Mac washed the car with a hose attached to the house, and then he invited Merri to go for a ride. They drove to the nearest town so that Merri would get used to larger numbers of people living in a local area. They stopped for a meal at a restaurant where Merri could enjoy her favorite pizza. She had hers with six toppings, while Mac settled for sausage, onions, and mushrooms. Merri was pleased that she conversed easily with the waitress, even using a few contractions in her speech in imitation of Mac's speech style.

On their way home, Mac said, "You mingled with the waitress and other people in that restaurant very well. Were you relaxed while you talked with them, or did it feel stressful?"

"I was relaxed. The surface world is new to me, but people aren't. Don't forget that we spent time at NASA together a while ago. The only new thing is that I'm getting used to adding a few contractions to my speech patterns to sound informal."

"Great! Tomorrow, I'll take you on another adventure."

That evening, Mac called Maxine and asked whether she would be open to having a couple of visitors on the following day.

"If one of them is you, Mac, I'd be delighted."

"Merri and I will get there around ten o'clock in the morning, if that suits your schedule."

"You're bringing Merrilong? How exciting. I've wanted to meet her."

"When she's living on the surface, she's Merri Long. Mac summarized his program of making all the Hallywalooly people comfortable with blending into surface living."

"It's your program. That's amazing. You have really become part of their world."

"I'll tell you the full story when we get there tomorrow. I also have another future program that may interest you and even your husband Charles."

"I have a feeling your visit is going to shake up our lives. Mine has never been the same since I first met you."

"Careful, Maxine; you're happily married."

"Don't worry. Charles and I are inseparable. That's why your comment about having something for both of us sounds intriguing."

"Until tomorrow morning, then."

The next morning, Mac and Merri arrived at Maxine's house promptly at ten o'clock.

As they parked, Merri said, "This house is much bigger than ours. Do Maxine and Charles have many children living with them?"

"They don't have any children."

"Why would two people need such a large house?"

"They don't need it that large, but Charles, as a bank vice president, wants people to be impressed with his success."

"That sounds wasteful."

"It is, and we'll talk more about it later, but just accept it for today, and enjoy your visit."

"A visit here is something you prepare for. In Hallywalooly, we simply stand outside someone's home until they invite us in."

"It is a bit different here. Advance notice allows the host or hostess time to prepare."

"What do they prepare?"

"Let's go inside and see."

Maxine greeted them at the front door and announced that Charles had stayed home from work in order to meet them. She ushered Mac and Merri into the glass-enclosed garden room where a wide assortment of pastries, fruit, and cheeses adorned a glass-topped table.

Charles stood from his perch on a stool at the bar, where he was drinking coffee. "Welcome. I've wanted to meet Mac for a long time, and it's a pleasant bonus to meet you, Merri."

Mac extended his hand for a firm handshake. "Same here, Charles. I've appreciated the occasional assistance you've given Maxine when I asked her for a favor."

Merri copied Mac and reached out for a handshake with Maxine, but Maxine surprised her with a kiss on the cheek. "Oh! That is a new custom for me. Very interesting."

Maxine laughed. "When we girls are alone together,

I'll coach you on when to do the cheek kiss and when to avoid it."

Mac turned to Charles. "Merri has recently arrived here and is continuing to learn our customs."

Merri stared at Charles in an odd way. "Mac, you don't have to cover for me, at least in this house. Charles Barkson is a Stopper. He has been sitting here worrying about whether I would detect him despite his trying to jam my thought reading. Anyway, knowing your status, I feel more relaxed with you, Charles."

Maxine's expression changed. "Charles! You never told me you were from Hallywalooly!"

Charles shrugged and sat on his barstool again. "Everyone relax. Before Hallywalooly had Topper agents like Maxine on the surface, they used Stoppers like me. There are just a few of us, and we don't contact each other. Once I met Maxine and fell in love with her, I asked Jablesh to make her an agent, so that I wouldn't have to keep worrying about her discovering my history. As an agent, she would hide her activities from me, and her secretiveness was my best defense."

Maxine said, "Not so fast, Charles. Why didn't you confide in me, even when I asked you to assist me in helping Mac?"

"I thought it would be easier to play the scene as the generous husband, willing to cooperate with the ex-boyfriend."

"There's more to it than that."

"Yes, Maxine. I was afraid you wouldn't want or love me if you knew I was a Stopper."

"Charles Barkson, you should have had more confidence in my love for you."

"How many times did I hear you talking about great

times with Mac?"

Mac stepped between them. "That's enough friction between you two. You've had some surprises this morning, but I think it's time for you to kiss and make up."

Maxine and Charles did exactly that.

Maxine invited her guests to take some food from her table assortment. "Please forgive us. That unexpected spat kept us from being good hosts. Anyway, I finally know why Charles is such a good banker. He can read a client's thoughts. I also know why he tries to make himself look older. He doesn't age the way I do."

Mac raised a quizzical eyebrow. "You know things about Stoppers that I didn't learn until I lived in Hallywalooly for quite a while."

Maxine blushed. "I guess both Charles and I had our secrets. I had a brief fling with Jablesh."

Merri laughed. "This is all very funny. You had a fling with my grandfather."

# CHAPTER 84 – CONTACT

After Merri and Mac returned home after their two-week surface residency, Merri said, "I'm going to miss sunrises and sunsets plus looking at the nighttime sky."

"You'll be back there soon, but it's time to give others a chance to experience surface living during this test period. Have your feelings about our underground home changed?"

"Of course not, Mac. The house we lived in for two weeks was a vacation. This is our home. I did like looking out windows. Perhaps we could have our computer screen show surface window-views when it is not in use for serious purposes."

"Good idea. You work on that while I check something out."

"Where are you going?"

"I didn't tell anyone, but Jablesh left a second communicator device for me hidden in a compartment in the wall of his home. I want to go over there to see whether it received any messages from him during his voyage to Titan, or from the Titan colony."

"I'll go with you."

Merri drove the utilizer cart with Mac as passenger. When they arrived at Jablesh's home, they went inside and Mac located the panel hiding the communicator compartment. He found three recorded messages. The first was from Jablesh.

*Greetings to everyone in Hallywalooly. We have entered orbit around Saturn's moon, Titan. Our journey went smoothly, although the Guardians and the three celebrity Droppers had some difficulties during our rapid accelerations and decelerations. We will orbit for several Titan days while I discuss our best landing site with the colony leadership. The atmosphere is opaque, so we will depend on guidance from the colonists to locate our appropriate landing spot.*

The second message, also from Jablesh, indicated some tension.

*We have landed on firm ground near Kraken Mare the sea near Titan's North Pole. The colonists treat us as aliens even though we are both descended from the same Ancient Ones. I will soon leave the ship to discuss with them NASA's plans and schedule. They have plenty of time to prepare or move before NASA comes, but initial discussions suggest they may not want to make any preparations at all.*

The third message was from a colony leader, speaking in the language of the Ancient Ones. Mac could understand it, but Merrilong could not.

*To the new leader of Hallywalooly, I bring sad news. Jablesh has died. He left the spacecraft to join us for discussions, assuming that he would be able to adapt to our nitrogen, ethane, and methane atmosphere as he had in ancient times adapted to the atmosphere of Earth. Old age diminished his capabilities, and he has succumbed. Jablesh will receive our traditional disposal of his body. The assistants and passengers that Jablesh brought with him are still well and living inside the spacecraft. We do not know how long they will survive in the craft's manufactured Earth atmosphere, and with its limited food supplies. We hope you will send instructions for disposal of their bodies.*

Mac translated the recording for Merrilong, who said he would have to formulate an answer soon.

Mac responded, "I can't reply, because I can understand their language, but I can't speak or write it. Summerly is the only one remaining in Hallywalooly who can send an answering message. Join me in concentrating our thoughts to request she come here."

"We could send a message through the computer to Hollywing and request that she relay it to Summerly."

"I'm not yet ready to share the news of Jablesh's death with additional people. Let's try the concentrated thought approach first. You've taught me that it is very powerful, especially when aimed at Summerly, who is extremely perceptive."

Mac and Merrilong agreed on a short summoning message and focused on sending it to Summerly. In case she wasn't alert enough to be maximally receptive, they repeated the thought message three times. Then they settled down to wait for a response.

The concentrated thought response arrived to both of them within five minutes. *"Coming."*

Twenty minutes later, Mac walked to the entrance to invite Summerly inside.

Following the customary greetings, Mac detailed the messages they had received and explained to Summerly that she was the only one who could respond to the colonists on Titan.

"Actually, Mac, you could do it with a little advanced training. I'll save that for the future because we have an immediate problem."

Merrilong asked, "Is there anything we can do for those who are still alive on the spacecraft? Any kind of healing message you could send, or instructions for a healer in the Titan colony?"

"I doubt that they have anything like our Requisition Center that could make oxygen and a breathing apparatus for each of them, and they'd need the same Center to manufacture food that our people could digest. I suspect that Jablesh knew the Droppers would not survive on Titan and had only a hope that the Stopper Guardians would."

Merrilong said, "Perhaps the Guardians can adapt to the Titan atmosphere. They are much younger than Jablesh."

"I will ask them to let one Guardian volunteer to try breathing their atmosphere, but we still have the problems of extreme cold and some suitable food to eat. The typical temperature there is -290 degrees Fahrenheit or -179 degrees Celsius. I suspect the Titan colonists have survived by eating things that would be totally incompatible with the human digestive system. Our passengers won't have time to adapt to such unusual nutrition."

Mac disagreed. "Jablesh would not be so cruel or careless as to take Hallywalooly people to Titan without a plan for feeding them. Further, Shorty and his Guardians are capable of designing and building sophisticated devices. They are our resources there, not just marooned passengers. The colonists thrive in the cold. If they work together with Shorty and his group of Guardians, they should be able to find ways to let our people continue living aboard the spacecraft indefinitely."

Summerly said, "That's intriguing thinking, Mac.

What would you have me do?"

"First, contact Shorty by responding to one of Jablesh's messages, and present your plan for testing one volunteer Guardian for adaptability to breathing the Titan atmosphere. This might even be accomplished without leaving the spacecraft if the volunteer sits in the exit airlock, open to the atmosphere. You may want to have a colonist healer standing by for emergencies."

"The healer could be in the airlock with the volunteer."

"Good thinking. The next project should be to teach someone on board the spacecraft to speak the ancient language of the colonists so that the two groups can communicate with each other. That will require ongoing efforts on your part."

Summerly gestured her agreement. "I will do that."

Mac turned to Merrilong. "You'll have a very important part to play in this effort. Get together with Hollywing at the Intelligence Center, and research how surface firms are producing animal feeds from methane. I remember seeing an article on the internet about that. Once you learn their process, you'll have to take it further to make the manufactured food suitable for Stoppers and Droppers to eat."

Merri smiled her agreement. "Now, I'll get to show you how good I am at engineering and science. I'll take the utilizer and get started right away. You can go home with Summerly."

"Be sure to tell Hollywing to keep Jablesh's death secret until we're ready to share that news."

"Right." Merrilong left for the Intelligence Center.

"Summerly, when you contact Shorty, tell him that

some of the Titan rock formations may be frozen water ice and that NASA thinks there is a water ocean deep beneath it. The spacecraft has the capability of breaking down water molecules to get hydrogen for fuel. It normally discards the oxygen from that breakdown. He can work on equipment for storing the oxygen released during that process. Then ask the colonists whether they have any way of getting liquid water from the underground ocean."

"Jablesh had great faith in your leadership abilities, Mac. You are doing a good job at defining the tasks we will have to do, both here and on Titan."

"Defining tasks is easy. Accomplishing them is much harder. We'll be counting on you to handle the communications and ancient language training."

"I will get started right away."

# CHAPTER 85
# – JABLESH

Once everyone working on solutions to the distant problems of Titan crew members initiated their research and communication efforts, Mac met with Hollywing to discuss the best way to announce Jablesh's death. As usual, they met in the Intelligence Center's Secure Room Number One. Hollywing made sure there was plenty of coffee for Mac. She added an extra mug for herself because the aroma had pleased her during prior meetings.

Hollywing sipped her coffee once they had settled in their seats. "I think I'll be joining you for coffee from now on. It's quite enjoyable."

Mac emptied his mug in three extended gulps and set it down on the table. "And you've taken your transition lessons seriously, Holly. You're using contractions and speaking informally. How shall we handle the announcement of Jablesh's death?"

"Thanks for the compliment. Traditionally, we just have a matter-of-fact announcement, and then move on to normal activities while aiming caring thoughts at the deceased person."

"For many years, in fact centuries, Jablesh was the motivator for everything that went on in Hallywalooly.

Surely, he should receive some special recognition upon his passing."

"He was the motivator because he was the guide to all the traditions of the Ancient Ones. He did not have an official leadership position. The tradition he would have followed is the simple announcement plus well-wishing projected thoughts."

"Fair enough, Holly, but there is another tradition of the Ancient Ones that suggests we should do something special."

"What other tradition?"

"Summerly told me that the voyage to Titan was Jablesh's heroic quest in the face of his diminishing capabilities and expected death. She said that on the original home planet, if one completed such a major quest with reliable witnesses, that person's life became woven into the ancestral tapestry of legends. Jablesh fulfilled his quest by traveling to Titan to aid the colony there. He is now a legend and must receive the affirmations of the people."

"Damn it, Mac! You've absorbed our traditions better than most of us Stoppers."

"And you've absorbed surface speech patterns, including exclamations really well. So, what should we do to honor Jablesh?"

"How about putting up a plaque or a statue that recognizes him as the Founder of Hallywalooly?"

"The statue would be perfect, especially in light of plans I'll propose for the future of Hallywalooly."

# CHAPTER 86 – FEEDBACK

Merrilong's excitement showed in her face when she returned from her second day working at the Intelligence Center on her project. "We can handle the food problem for the Guardian Stoppers and the celebrity Droppers on the spacecraft. I'm sure of it. The process in your article relies on methane-eating bacteria in vats feeding on the methane, giving them energy to reproduce tremendously. The bacteria and their waste products are collected and compressed into pellets for animal feed."

Mac held up his hand in a *stop* gesture. "Two questions. How do we know there are methane-eating bacteria on Titan, and how do you go from animal feed to human food?"

"This may sound a bit unpleasant, but we know there are bacteria on Titan, because we have colonists from our home planet, and like all creatures, they have waste products from their bodies that include bacteria. The question remains as to whether those bacteria feed on methane. Through the Intelligence Center, I located the oldest Stopper in Hallywalooly with the fewest ancestral cross-breedings with surface humans in order to come close to someone with the bodily functions of a Titan colonist. Samples of her waste material tested positive for bacteria, and they survived and thrived in a laboratory methane atmosphere. So, it's safe to assume there are methane-eating bacteria on Titan."

"Assuming that lets you make animal feed pellets, how do you get from there to people food?"

"By itself, the process might require additional development time, but as long as we find enough water on Titan for drinking and to be broken down into hydrogen to keep fueling the spacecraft and oxygen for breathing by the Hallywalooly passengers, we can mix the methane feed with vegetables grown on the spacecraft from seeds that Jablesh stowed on board in case they would be useful."

"I didn't know they had seeds."

"That information came in a message from Shorty yesterday."

"Great work, Merri. Have you learned anything about water availability?"

"Not yet, Mac. Summerly would get that information from the colonists. So far, she's the only one who can communicate with them."

"I'll check with her. Do you want to come along?"

"Not now. I want to check on how well the Requisition Center is running since we last repaired it. I'm not sure it will function smoothly forever."

# CHAPTER 87 – SUMMERLY

When Mac entered Summerly's healing studio, she was preparing a lesson recording for teaching passengers on the spacecraft the language of the Titan colonists. He waited in the other room until she finished.

When he no longer heard her voice, Mac entered her treatment room. "How are the lessons going?"

"I think we are making progress. This recording was my third lesson. So far, Shorty plus Eleanor Roosevelt and Benjamin Franklin are working on the language. I send them lesson recordings, which take a long time to arrive because of the great distance. Then they record their answers to my questions and repetitions of my sentences and send them back to me. Ben appears to be making the most rapid progress, which makes sense because he served as a diplomat in France during his first lifetime. He had to rapidly acquire fluency in French, and now he is doing the same with the colonists' language. By the way, I made extra copies of my language lesson recordings for you. You should be able to substitute for me if I am not available when Titan communications come through."

"Have you received any information from the colonists about the availability of water there?"

"Water ice is available, but given the extremely cold temperatures, large amounts of energy would be required to melt it to its liquid state. I have asked the colonists whether they know of underground liquid water lakes, but they have not yet replied."

"That's at least somewhat promising. If we can melt a small amount of the water ice and break it down into hydrogen and oxygen, we might be able to ignite methane or ethane from the lakes and atmosphere to burn with the oxygen and melt more water ice."

"Someone will have to do an analysis of the quantities of oxygen liberated and required. If you burn ethane or methane with insufficient oxygen, you get soot, which will make it even harder for our spacecraft passengers to breathe."

"Thanks, Summerly. I hadn't thought of that. I'll ask Merrilong to look into that analysis, but our best hope is that the colonists find a deep underground liquid water source."

"Before you leave, Mac, I must report that they were unsuccessful in their experiment to see whether the Guardian Stoppers could adapt to breathing the Titan atmosphere. They put a volunteer into the spacecraft's airlock along with a healer from the colonists. When the nitrogen/methane/ethane atmosphere was vented into the airlock, the volunteer started to suffocate. The healer saved him and purged the Titan atmosphere out of the airlock."

# CHAPTER 88 – PLANNING

As Mac sat doing computer work, Merrilong walked behind him and started to give him a back and shoulder massage.

"Oh, that feels good. Thanks, but don't stop. Keep it up for a couple of minutes more."

"You've done this to me more than a few times, Mac, and I enjoyed it. I never had a backrub before you came."

"I hope, on balance, I've added positive things to your life."

"I lived a long time before I met you, but my best memories are the ones we created together."

"Merri, you're getting to be a romantic. That's unusual for a Stopper."

"And how many Stoppers have you been intimate with?"

"Only you; you're more than enough."

"Thanks. What are you working on? Is it something to help the spacecraft passengers on Titan?"

"Not this time. Once Summerly gets them speaking the ancient language, I think they'll do well enough in cooperation with the colonists. I'm working on plans for Hallywalooly. We've already learned how to live and communicate better with the surface people, but I want to create something that will keep most of us connected to each other and to our underground world once some of us start living on the surface. I also want us to have cash resources to last well into the future."

"That sounds like a major project. I'm wondering what will happen when Stoppers start living on the surface and people there start to realize we're different. That could cause big problems. On the other hand, you now speak of yourself as a Stopper would, so if the transition works in one direction, it should succeed the other way around."

Mac swiveled around to face Merri. "I agree with you, but I'm counting on the fact that there are so many varieties of unusual surface people that Stoppers will never appear to be weirder than they are."

"Would anyone consider me weird?"

Mac hugged Merri. "They'd be too busy admiring your beauty."

"Would all of us Stoppers be expected to take jobs working for surface people?"

"Some would; the ones who wanted to move far away and be independent. Most of the Stoppers will work for Hallywalooly under my plan."

"What does that mean, Mac? No one works for Hallywalooly now."

"Not so, Merri. Many Stoppers, Droppers, and Toppers work for Hallywalooly now. They just don't get involved with cash payments. Guardians, Intelligence Center agents, agricultural workers, and the rest of us, all work to keep Hallywalooly going and improve it. We all have responsibilities and make contributions, even that old Stopper you tested for methane-eating bacteria."

"You're right as usual. I was simply worrying a bit about the unknown things that will face us in the future."

"That's natural. I'm sure we'll all handle new developments well. My plans will require additional training for some people, but they'll keep most of us within our comfortable surroundings on a regular basis."

"Those are all intriguing hints, but are you going to tell me exactly what you want to do?"

"Read my papers, and tell me whether you are willing to do what I suggest. Next, I'll schedule meetings with key people to learn whether I can build a consensus to go ahead with it."

Merrilong skimmed the papers. Then she gave him a hug. "I agree, and I almost think you're doing this just for me. I love it."

# CHAPTER 89 – PREPARATIONS

Hollywing had Secure Room Number One supplied with coffee and ready for use when he arrived. "Our meetings are getting to be more frequent and always interesting. What do we have to discuss this morning?"

"Several things, but first a bit of status checking. Have all the Stoppers who were interested taken their turns living in the surface houses?"

"Everyone who was willing has had an above-ground vacation with generally satisfactory results. A few Stoppers were not willing to participate, and we didn't force them to do so."

"Good. Have we made progress toward the statue of Jablesh?"

"We're reviewing the pictures we have of him from his appearances on our computer network. Once we make a final selection, we'll use it to create a statue through the Requisition Center. We haven't made Jablesh's death general knowledge yet, but we should soon, because rumors are spreading, some of them quite fantastic."

"Thank you, Hollywing. I always know I can depend on you and your Intelligence Center."

"What is the new plan? Merrilong told me you have

something major in mind."

"I do, and your group will have a very large part in it. My problem is that I need a large number of people to agree to the project before I can announce it. The outline of the venture is contained in these papers."

Hollywing took the stack of papers and read them carefully. "This is a great idea, Mac. We'll continue to fully utilize Hallywalooly while mingling comfortably with the surface people, and we'll generate income too. Count our group in. I'll select some individuals for you to consider for assignments."

"I hoped you would have that reaction. I'll need to have meetings with many others in order to get a sufficient group on board. I'll let you know when we're ready to proceed."

# CHAPTER 90 – SHORTY

When Mac checked the communicator in Jablesh's old home, he found a lengthy message from Shorty.

*Greetings from Titan, Mac. I am beginning to be able to converse with the colonists in the ancient language, thanks to Summerly's lessons. The colonists are mining incredibly hard water ice for us from rock-like surface outcroppings. They deliver it to our spacecraft's airlock. We built a combustion chamber for melting the water ice, using atmospheric methane for fuel. It requires that we insert a bit of our oxygen to allow combustion. After the water ice melts, we have liquid water for drinking and to break down into hydrogen for spacecraft fuel to keep our systems going and oxygen for breathing. We use some oxygen for combustion in the chamber, but get some back from the water we produce. It is a balancing procedure. So far our process is not sufficiently efficient to produce more oxygen than we use for combustion. We will try to improve it, but our hope is that the colonists will be able to locate the underground sea that NASA predicts. If they can tap into that, we will have unlimited supplies of oxygen and water. We have ample oxygen from on-board supplies for now, but we are doing all we can to conserve it by cutting it off in unused sections of the ship. I will keep you informed of future developments.*

Mac appreciated the resourcefulness of Shorty and the others on board the spacecraft, but he realized there was a chance that they would run out of oxygen before they improved the efficiency of their water ice reduction process or found a source of liquid water. He made a mental note to discuss the problem with Merri. He was always impressed by her technical creativity.

Mac thought for a few minutes and then sent a return message to Shorty.

*Congratulations on your work done so far to get liquid water, hydrogen, and oxygen from water ice. Congratulations also for learning how to communicate with the colonists. We will attempt to develop suggestions for improving your water ice reduction process. How is your food supply? Are you growing vegetables from your seeds or discovering colonist foods that you can eat? Merrilong is working on harvesting food from methane- eating bacteria. We will send test results and procedures soon.*

He wasn't at all sure that Merrilong would come up with a prototype factory process for making food from bacteria, but he wanted to give Shorty and the other spacecraft passengers some positive news. They knew their flight to Titan would be risky, but, working together, they would do everything possible to keep the spacecraft passengers alive and communicating with the colonists.

# CHAPTER 91 – CONSENSUS

Mac continued contacting key people about his long-term proposal for Hallywalooly and his recommendations for their roles in the project. He was pleasantly surprised by their almost unanimous endorsement of his efforts.

After satisfying himself that his project was indeed practical, he scheduled a meeting with Red, Hollywing, and Merrilong at the Intelligence Center. Once they had gathered, he presented new drawings and other documents to each of them.

"Thank you for coming. I feel that we have a consensus on going ahead with my proposal. Now we have many preliminary tasks to accomplish before it becomes reality. Red, the bulk of the efforts will involve you and your Guardians making physical changes to Hallywalooly. The sketches I gave you indicate my suggestions. You will want to translate the sketches into finished drawings and perhaps add your own additional construction details."

Red nodded his agreement. "Everything looks reasonable. I have some additional ideas, but some of them can wait until later as upgrades, rather than initial requirements."

"I'll let you decide the sequence of projects. Just be sure the three sketches marked with a star are completed first."

"I wondered what the stars meant."

"Hollywing, as you'll note from the list I gave you, we will require a major amount of paperwork, all keyed to referenced supporting sources. Can your computer and graphics people handle that?"

"Absolutely, Mac. We have been training for this type of effort for years. We're also ready to take on the ongoing responsibilities you indicate at the bottom of your list."

"Good. Merri, you'll have a project that I'm not even sure is possible."

"That's my favorite kind of assignment. What do you want me to do?"

"With support from Red's Guardians, I'd like you to figure out how we can move the Requisition Center to a remote and secret location. If you can't do that, we'll have to build something over it that hides it or disguises its function."

"You're right. That will be a difficult job. The Requisition Center is very complex, but I'll analyze it and come up with a workable proposal."

"Thanks, Merri. The guidelines for the Requisition Center will apply to all of our projects. If our initial approach is too difficult or impossible, we'll have to come up with an alternate way to achieve our goal in each case. Let me know when you propose to do a task in an unusual but creative way. That's all I have for now. Thanks for your efforts."

# CHAPTER 92 – ANNOUNCEMENTS

The preparations required several months, but the day finally arrived when the computer screens made several key announcements:

*We regret having to announce the death of our great leader and motivator, Jablesh, during his distant mission. A statue of him will soon be on display. Its location will be announced soon.*

*The Requisition Center has been closed prior to its move to a new location. All requisitions should be submitted to the Intelligence Center from this time forward.*

*The Guardians announce the completion of our new residential village on the surface. You may submit suggestions for naming it. During the next month, most Hallywalooly residents will be relocated in new permanent village housing. This will allow the Guardians to perform additional necessary renovations of our underground chambers. Upon moving to the village, all Hallywalooly residents will use their new surface names and will be issued corresponding identification documents.*

*Additional announcements, including individual assignments, will be made upon the Guardians' completion of our underground renovations.*

Mac smiled after reading the announcements. The

plan was being realized on a step-by-step basis. He took special notice of the second announcement. "Merrilong, you found a way to move the Requisition Center?"

"It hasn't been moved yet, but I'm working with Red on a plan."

"Are you going to dismantle it piece-by-piece and then reassemble it?"

"No. There would be too many opportunities for errors."

"What are you going to do?"

"The Requisition Center was constructed over a pit, so that pipes, tubes, wires, and shuttling mechanisms could be located in the space beneath it. We're going to jack up the whole structure and construct a substitute *pit* on heavy duty wheels beneath it. Then we'll be able to tow the entire Requisition Center to any desired location."

"Very clever, but you won't be able to conceal it in a location that doesn't have wide access routes."

"To the contrary, Mac. Red's people are going to tow the unit up the ramp to the surface and then lower it through the clamshell doors into the spacecraft launch cavern. The spacecraft is not likely to return, and even if it did, there's a side chamber large enough for the Requisition Center. The Guardians will cover and camouflage the clamshell doors, of course, after the transfer is complete."

"That's great thinking. The only access would be through Jablesh's old home, and the connecting passageway was hidden by him a long time ago. The Requisition Center will remain functional but hidden so well that no visitors from the surface will ever find it. That's important, because its technology is so advanced that visitors might suspect Hallywalooly's history."

"Mac, we'll have to be sure that none of our Stoppers, Droppers, and Toppers reveal our true nature in casual conversations."

"I'm counting on making it clear to everyone that the consequences of such a revelation would be devastating to all of us."

# CHAPTER 93 – PUBLICITY

No one knew how the surface population would respond to the initial news releases sent out from the Intelligence Center, but thanks in part to agents Hollywing had planted on the staffs of key publications, articles started to appear in the press, complete with enticing cavern photographs. Soon, social media created a buzz too.

*Hallywalooly College of Planetary Studies Opening for Fall Semester*

*Florida's Hallywalooly College is the first underground institution dedicated to studies of planet Earth and its further evolution. Courses are aimed at learning to live compatibly with the planet's needs during this era of climate change. Innovative technology courses emphasize the effects of human lifestyles and economics on the environment. The underground campus provides the student with an up-close-and-personal sensitivity to our planet's structure and processes.*

*Faculty and Staff*
- *Founder: J. Ablesh (deceased)*
- *President: Malcolm Blackwell*
- *Administrative Vice President: Holly Winger*
- *Dean of Students: Paul Cooper*

- *Engineering and Technology: Merri Long*
- *Geology and Civil Engineering: Connor O'Rourke*
- *Mineralogy: Flora O'Brien*
- *Environmental Science: Patty Chambers*
- *Psychology and the History of Medicine: Summer Lee*
- *Dramatics and Stagecraft: Paula Jenkins*
- *Economics: Charles Barkson*
- *Lifestyles and Consumerism: Maxine Barkson*
- *Conflict Resolution: Paul Cooper*

When Merrilong examined the list of faculty and staff, she told Mac it looked very impressive. "I know all these people. My only problem is that I don't remember all the name changes for surface living. Some are obvious, but others elude me."

"No problem. J. Ablesh is Jablesh. Holly Winger is Hollywing. Paul Cooper is Preacher Clark. You, of course, are Merri Long ..."

"And soon I'll be Merri Blackwell when we marry."

"Right. Connor O'Rourke is Red. Flora O'Brien is Flowerling, Red's mate ..."

"And she'll get married as Flora O'Rourke."

"Right again. Patty Chambers is Trisha. I never knew her last name."

"It was a hard one to remember."

"Summer Lee was, of course, Summerly, and Paula Jenkins is Trisha's friend, Phyllis Jennings. Charles and Maxine Barkson have not changed their names. They're already surface people."

"And Charles is proof that a Stopper can easily blend in with surface people. It is amusing to see that you have Preacher, I mean Paul Cooper, teaching Conflict

Resolution."

"He's changed his outlook completely since becoming a Dropper and dwelling with the Stoppers of Hallywalooly. Proving himself to Trisha also taught him about that subject. So, there you have it. Hallywalooly is now a college, and we will live and work with topsiders both above and below ground."

"What about those Stoppers and Droppers who want to move away and live on the surface all the time?"

"They won't have any problems, Merri, so long as they follow the caution rules we taught them. Their identification papers will be accepted, and they'll be treated just like everyone else."

"I wonder how surface people will feel if they ever discover some of their neighbors had ancestors from another part of the galaxy."

"Many surface people already have neighbors who are much stranger than residents of Hallywalooly."

"I'll have to get together with the others who will teach engineering and technology subjects and develop a curriculum for each subject."

"We'll have major work preparing for our first class of students, but my guess is that they'll be so amazed by their Hallywalooly surroundings that most of our time will be spent answering questions."

# CHAPTER 94 – OPENING DAY

Anne Brownly and her half-brother, Bill Trioni, climbed down from Bill's old red Ford pickup truck with its blue replacement tailgate, riding high on its oversized tires. They scanned the parking lot and were impressed by the large number of people walking from their cars and trucks toward the warehouse-style administration building. That blocky building bore a lighted Hallywalooly College of Planetary Studies sign and a cloth banner beneath it emblazoned, *Welcome Students*.

Anne and Bill had applied without knowing the size of the institution just because they wanted careers in some field that would help the future of Planet Earth. Apparently, many other people of various ages felt the same way.

Inside the administration building, they saw a circle of counters surrounding a statue of a man wearing a garment that looked like a monk's robe. Anne and Bill joined the line leading to a counter underneath a sign reading *STEP 1*. That line shortened quickly, and they soon found themselves facing a woman wearing a badge labeled *Holly Winger*. She checked off their names against her admissions list on her computer screen.

Then she smiled and said, "I see you both have the same address and already paid for your first semester. You may skip the cashier's counter at *STEP 2*, and go to the one marked *STEP 3*, where you will receive your class schedule. We have the same general courses for all students during their first semester. In future semesters, you will be encouraged to select a specialty or two and take individualized courses. When you receive your schedule, you will be assigned rooms in our aboveground dormitory. Everyone this year is a freshman and must either commute or live in the dormitory. Starting in your junior year, you may qualify to stay in an underground apartment. Do you have any questions so far?"

Bill asked, "Is it true that the whole campus is underground?"

"Yes, you will have all your classes underground except for a few field trips."

Anne asked, "Will there be any part-time jobs available for students?"

"There will be some in the dormitory, and we will be developing additional jobs underground which will be listed, as available, in this building. After you receive your schedule and dormitory assignment, head for the sign that says *STEP 4* where you will board shuttle cars we call utilizers that will take you down a ramp to our underground campus. Once there, you will receive an introductory tour. Your classes will start tomorrow."

After Anne and Bill left, Holly saw Mac approaching, so she asked an assistant to continue welcoming students while she had a discussion with him.

"Well, Mr. President, the college concept is working better than I ever expected. The Guardians may have to build a second dormitory."

"Didn't you place a limit on admissions?"

"Our target was four hundred students, but after we put out some news releases and public relations announcements, we received more than five thousand applications. I discussed our capability for accommodating more students with Red, or I should say Connor O'Rourke, and he said that he had built an expansion margin into his rework of the caverns. Based on his figures, I raised the class size to five hundred."

"You do realize that means a student body of two thousand when these freshmen get to be seniors."

"Yes, Mac, but during their four years, we'll keep adapting additional caverns for teaching use and special purposes. Don't worry. The Guardians can work continuously in areas that are off-limits to the students."

"I was a student once, and I doubt that they'll obey the rules as well as Stoppers and Droppers have in the past."

"Agreed, but the Guardians will be watchful. The student orientation manual subtly threatens expulsion if there are discipline problems. Beyond that, you know that we can use our mind control capabilities on trouble-makers."

"You're right, Holly. I keep thinking of our college as a more conventional institution but, if we're careful, we can use mind control and healing techniques without their realizing that anything unusual is happening. Who are the tour guides once the students get down the ramp to the lower level?"

"We're depending on our former Droppers to handle that. They're all energized after you and Summerly made them fully alive again. They also can relate to the students as former topsiders themselves."

"I hope the former gang members and others with unusual backgrounds retained their disciplined Dropper outlooks when we gave them a second chance to be fully alive."

"I haven't seen any problems, and Preacher; that is Paul Cooper; is keeping an eye on them. I really should do a better job of remembering all the new names."

"It won't be long before they're completely natural to you, Holly – at least I hope so."

Mac drove his utilizer down the ramp and located Red. "Everything looks great, Connor. I have just one potential problem that's been bothering me."

"You can keep calling me Red, Mac. Connor O'Rourke can go by his nickname among friends. I've enjoyed having our crews make all the modifications. What's your potential problem?"

"For the time being, we're still going to have some Stoppers living in their old homes, and Summer will want her studio off-limits to students. We've never used doors to keep our chambers private. We need to keep students from entering homes and offices where they don't belong."

"I've been thinking about that. Wooden doors are possible, but difficult to fit within stone entrance openings of various shapes. How about tough rubberized inflatable plugs that inflate and deflate with a control like a garage door opener? Each would be matched to its individual opening size but would inflate to fill irregular entrance shapes."

"That sounds good. How long would it take to fit them to at least the private chambers?"

"If we use our hidden Requisition Center to obtain

the inflatable plugs, the pumps, and the remote controls, we should be able to start on them today. I'll assign a team to obtain specifications for each opening and feed that data into the Requisition Center computers."

"Great. Do the private entrances before you plug the doorways to classrooms, lecture halls, and laboratories."

As Mac drove by new classrooms and other facilities, he monitored the thoughts of students on their orientation tours as he passed them. He was surprised to learn that many of them were thinking about food facilities and made a mental note to add one or more conventional fast food outlets in addition to his restaurant supported by the Requisition Center. He thought ahead three years to the point where they would have two thousand students plus faculty and staff. Feeding all those people multiple times every day would be a huge task.

When he returned home, he found Merri finalizing the lesson plans for her department for the next day. "You appear to be in complete control. Any nervousness about becoming an academic?"

"Not in the slightest, Mac. It should be fun and a creative change from centuries of hiding from the surface folks in Hallywalooly. Now we'll feel comfortable with them, and they won't realize there's anything different about us."

"Good outlook. Next week we'll be moving to our permanent house on the surface. It will be two blocks from the dormitory, so we'll be seen as living on-campus, but we'll have enough separation from the students to have some privacy."

"I'm sure I'll like that, Mac. Right now, I'll have to distract you from college opening thoughts. Just before you arrived, we received a notice that you have a new message from Shorty on Titan. You should go to Jablesh's former home to receive it and reply."

"Will do. I feel a bit guilty for concentrating on the college opening and putting the Titan adventure in the back of my mind."

# CHAPTER 95
# – SHORTY

Once at Jablesh's former home, Mac removed the communication unit from behind its concealing panel. He pressed the button opposite the flashing light, and Shorty's message appeared on the screen.

*Greetings, Mac. The latest developments here on Titan are sad, but not completely unexpected. Our celebrity Droppers, Ben Franklin, Eleanor Roosevelt, and Orville Wright, have all died. They required more oxygen than we have been able to produce from our processing of the Titan frozen water ice rock fragments. Their dying changed our requirements so that we can now produce adequate amounts of oxygen and water for the rest of us. We have also modified the colonists' foods with the help of their technology people so that we can consume them and they provide us with adequate nutrition. Tell Merrilong that we won't need the artificial food she was developing. Hallywalooly food was much better, but we're now sure we can survive here for as long as required. Do you want us to conduct any special observance for the dead celebrity Droppers or to dispose of their bodies in a significant way?*

Mac pondered Shorty's last question for several minutes. Then he smiled and responded.

*Do you have enough fuel to launch the spacecraft*

*again? If so, travel from Saturn's Titan moon to its Enceladus moon and do the following ...*

*Then return to Titan and continue your stay with the colonists until such time as they or you choose to move elsewhere.*

Mac replaced the communicator unit in its hidden compartment and headed home. He felt sure that Merri would share his laughter over what he had done. It might cause consternation in some quarters, but it would fulfill Jablesh's mission of letting the Titan colonists live in peace.

# CHAPTER 96
# – NASA

Jerry Arkinthorpe, elevated to Project Manager of the Enceladus Orbiter Mission, bristled when Mission Specialist Sandra Markie barged into his office without knocking. "I'm preparing for my presentation to Congress. I can't be disturbed."

"Sorry, Jerry, but you'll want to see the latest orbiter photos. They're unbelievable if our interpretation is correct."

Jerry followed Sandra to the control room, disturbed that they needed his personal attention for almost everything. "This had better be important."

Once in the control room, he stared up at the giant display. At first he saw nothing unusual. Then Sandra aimed her laser pointer at an area near the bottom of the display. Three identical perfect rectangles were outlined side-by-side, carved into the surface ice.

Jerry stared at the screen. "Those are significant. Straight lines and right angles don't appear naturally on a moon or planet."

Sandra said, "There's more to those outlines than that, Jerry."

"What do you mean?"

"We calculated the dimensions of those outlines.

The rectangles are approximately the standard size for grave openings."

"Damn! That must mean the Russians or the Chinese beat us again. I'm going to request that we delay the Titan missions and focus all our Saturn moon efforts on Enceladus. I'm sure we'll get unlimited funding, now that we know we're chasing the Russians and Chinese."

-END-

# ABOUT THE AUTHOR

## Richard M. Davidson

Richard Davidson, who adds his middle initial for science fiction works (think Mind-stretching), as he begins his Hallywalooly Series with Stoppers, is the author of the self-help guidebook, DECISION TIME! Better Decisions for a Better Life. He has written the five-volume Lord's Prayer Mystery Series: Lead Us Not into Temptation, Give Us this Day Our Daily Bread, Forgive Us Our Trespasses, Thy Will Be Done, and Deliver Us from Evil. He has edited an anthology, Overcoming. His Imp Mystery Series includes six novels: Implications, Impulses, Impostor, Impending, Impasse, and Loyalties. He has also written six Lentren Bible Studies in the Email Jesus Series; a self-help gift book, Slimmericks; and a childhood memoir, After the Storm. Mr. Davidson is President Emeritus of Off-Campus Writers' Workshop, the oldest ongoing group of its kind in the U,S.A. He is a former Lay Leader in the United Methodist Church. Mr. Davidson is an aeronautical & astronautical engineer.

# ACKNOWLEDGEMENT

Every author needs feedback and encouragement from peers in the writing community, both formal and informal. I especially want to thank the members of my Critique Group: Brenda, Sarah, Estelle, Kelley, Judy, Peter, Lyle, and Barry. They have endorsed my writing while acting as a spectrum of readers, frequently seeing discrepancies I overlooked. They have also become a family of close friends. Collectively, they have written many fine articles and books in many genres, most of which I proudly keep in my personal library.

# BOOKS BY THIS AUTHOR

**Decision Time!**

**Overcoming**

**Slimmericks**

**Lead Us Not Into Temptation**

**Give Us This Day Our Daily Bread**

**Forgive Us Our Trespasses**

**Thy Will Be Done**

**Deliver Us From Evil**

# Stoppers

www.ingramcontent.com/pod-product-compliance
Lightning Source LLC
Chambersburg PA
CBHW051237260626
47162CB00002B/478

* 9 7 8 0 9 9 7 6 3 8 1 7 2 *